THE ANNALS OF
SHERLOCK HOLMES

This sparkling collection of three new Sherlock Holmes stories draw on details and hints from the pages of Conan Doyle's classic works. From the pen of the acclaimed Doctor John Watson we are introduced to previously unsolved mysteries as referenced in many of the original stories.

Books by Paul D. Gilbert
Published by The House of Ulverscroft:

SHERLOCK HOLMES AND THE GIANT
RAT OF SUMATRA

PAUL D. GILBERT

THE ANNALS OF SHERLOCK HOLMES

Complete and Unabridged

ULVERSCROFT
Leicester

First published in Great Britain in 2012 by
Robert Hale Limited
London

First Large Print Edition
published 2013
Robert Hale Limited
London

A catalogue record for this book is available
from the British Library.

ISBN 978–1–4448–1713–3

Published by
F. A. Thorpe (Publishing)
Anstey, Leicestershire

Set by Words & Graphics Ltd.
Anstey, Leicestershire
Printed and bound in Great Britain by
T. J. International Ltd., Padstow, Cornwall

This book is printed on acid-free paper

I would like to dedicate this collection to John Hale for the continuing faith and trust that he has shown me, and to my friends and colleagues who are campaigning for a posthumous BAFTA for my hero, the late Jeremy Brett.

This book is also in memory of my later father-in-law who sadly passed away on the very day that it was accepted for publication and also in memory of Lois Grace, the brightest new star in the heavens.

As ever, my eternal gratitude goes to the world's number one Sherlockian, my wife Jackie.

P.D.G.

Contents

Foreword

It has been most gratifying for me to note how many favourable and positive reviews my last collection of Sherlock Holmes pastiches, *The Chronicles*, has received from both amateur and professional critics alike.

However, despite my best efforts at novelizing the tale of *Sherlock Holmes and the Giant Rat of Sumatra*, many of my fellow *Sherlockians* have pointed out that there is a vast wealth of potentially untapped literary treasures that still remain to be unearthed.

I am only too aware that many of these throwaway references were probably inserted with Sir Arthur Conan Doyle's tongue placed very firmly in his cheek! Nonetheless, a number of these, so called, unchronicled cases have proven to be irresistible to me. One notable reviewer has even dared me to tackle the *Dundas Separation Case*. So be it.

I was uncertain as to whether a volume comprising of three novellas, would be acceptable to the purists amongst you. However, on closer examination, I soon realized that, with the exception of *The Hound of the Baskervilles*, each one of Doyle's full length novels were no more than a hundred pages in length.

I sincerely hope that I have been able to rise to these fresh challenges in a manner that you will find both satisfactory and enjoyable.

1

THE DUNDAS
SEPARATION CASE

' . . . *This is the Dundas separation case . . . he had drifted into the habit of winding up every meal by taking out his false teeth and hurling them at his wife . . .* '
(*A Case of Identity* by A. Conan Doyle)

' . . . *I have Mr Holmes's authority for saying that the whole story of the politician, the lighthouse and the trained cormorant will be given to the public . . .* '
(*The Veiled Lodger* by A. Conan Doyle)

PART ONE

The Politician

A light flurry of snow darted arbitrarily as it fell against the background of a pale grey winter sky. When it did eventually reach the ground, it provided a white dusting to the broad expanse of lawn that was spread before us.

Every so often the shimmering moon peeked out from behind the drifting, broken clouds and illuminated the tiny flakes as they were gradually transformed into a brocade of ice. Occasionally the fine snow was picked up by a cruel, unforgiving wind and churned around into a spectral whirlpool.

The mere sight was enough to send a violent shudder through to my very core and induced me to pull my coat collar as high as it would go. My friend, Sherlock Holmes, was evidently aware of, and amused by, my discomfort.

'Oh, Watson, you allow yourself to dwell too much upon the chill outside rather than focusing upon the relative warmth within,' he chided me cheerily.

'I am not aware of any sort of warmth within!' I protested forcefully. I could not help but wonder at my friend's effrontery. After all, he was sitting comfortably in the corner of this tiny stable with his muffler tied down about his hat while a large brown blanket was draped over his shoulders forming the shape of a teepee.

'I can assure you that this is not exactly the Christmas Eve that I had anticipated!' I continued complaining.

My mind drifted back to the room that we had left behind in Baker Street. Our roaring fire had been in full glow and Mrs Hudson had festooned our walls with a profusion of green and red. There had been some most tempting smells wafting upwards from her kitchen and two mysterious parcels were upon our table.

'Is there anything of note?' Holmes asked hopefully as he reached his right hand under his coverings.

'It is certainly a lot colder and whiter than it was when we first arrived. However, the house is still in complete darkness and there are no signs of movement, neither inwards nor outwards,' I reported dejectedly.

'Well then, cheer yourself with this and I will continue the watch!' Holmes suddenly announced, while he produced a silver flask from within his blanket. This he offered to me with a smile.

'I could not contemplate a Christmas Eve without my Watson savouring a good measure of his favourite Cognac.'

I accepted this gratefully.

'It was very thoughtful of you,' I said, as I made my way into the slightly warmer corner of our hideout that Holmes had just vacated. He, in turn, relieved me of my vigil at the window.

Holmes appeared to be less affected by the cold than I had been. Obviously he had the advantage of his enormous blanket, but that was not all. He had a clearer understanding of our reason for being there and that, in itself, provided him with the diligence and steely intent that had enabled him to shut out all other thoughts. His eyes and his other senses would not deviate from their vigilance, even for a moment. As he sat there, with his long sharp features protruding from under the edge of his blanket, he reminded me of the statue of an ancient Egyptian jackal that I had viewed recently at the Bloomsbury museum. Although, perhaps, Holmes was displaying fewer signs of animation.

The golden liquid with which Holmes supplied me had an immediate warming effect and I sat there gratefully caressing the life-preserving flask. I had seen and heard everything that Holmes had. Therefore I decided to recollect, as vividly as I could, the events and the exact circumstances that had led us to our current predicament in the hope that I might benefit from the same under-standing as that of my friend.

One morning a few days before Christmas I had decided to return from a visit with my people in Goole, so that I might share the festivities with my old friend in Baker Street. As soon as I had turned the key in the front door I realized that I was to be sorely disappointed. A pile of holly sprigs, that Mrs Hudson was to have hung within our rooms, lay forlornly at the base of our stairs and our hapless landlady bustled out to greet me in a state of great agitation.

'Oh, Doctor! Thank goodness you have returned early. I really do not know what is wrong with Mr Holmes lately. He has been in one of his moods, almost from the very moment that you departed for Goole. I am afraid that there has been no reasoning with him at all. See here, he even bundled me out of his room before I had a chance to hang these!' The poor befuddled woman pointed down to the foliage by her feet.

I placed a reassuring hand upon her shoulder before removing and hanging up my hat and coat.

'Do not concern yourself, Mrs Hudson. I

am certain that Mr Holmes has been vexed by a troublesome case, or frustrated by an elusive clue and nothing of more serious note. I assure you that I shall speak to him this very instant and set things right.' I said this as I climbed determinedly up the stairs, although, in truth, Mrs Hudson was probably more convinced of my likely success than I was myself.

I decided to disrupt Holmes's reverie by barging into the room, unannounced and without ceremony. I might have crept silently towards him in my slippers, for all the difference that my clumsy intrusion provoked in him. He was sitting cross-legged upon his favourite chair with his purple dressing-gown tightly drawn around him. In itself that was quite understandable, for the fire had clearly not been drawn for many an hour and, as a consequence, our room was painfully cold.

Holmes's unlit pipe protruded from between his thin, dry lips and his tousled, unkempt hair fell over his eyebrows. His eyes flashed briefly in my direction and he emitted a faint, high-pitched grunt of acknowledgment, by way of a greeting.

'So, you have decided to return,' Holmes said listlessly.

I strode purposefully over to the windows and closed them with some vigour, in an effort to shut out the harsh December air. I then turned sternly towards my friend.

'I might have saved myself the effort!' I retorted. 'I cut short my visit to my people in Goole that I might spend a pleasant Christmas in my own rooms, here in Baker Street. I was then to discover our poor landlady forlorn at the base of the stairs. You might at least have allowed her to hang the holly and stoke the fire. It is like ice in here, Holmes.'

'It is a little sharp, I suppose,' Holmes conceded, whilst further tightening the cord around his dressing-gown.

'Sharp, indeed!' I exclaimed. 'I assume that your behaviour has been provoked by a lack of cases to keep you active?'

'I have told you often enough that to assume anything is a great failing, Watson. As a matter of fact I have seven or eight on the go at the moment and not one of them is worthy of a moment of my time!' he snapped aggressively, out of sheer frustration. 'What use are the powers which you so dramatically attribute to me, if I am to be constantly deluged with requests from schoolboys to find their lost puppies, or from young housemaids who are anxious to discover the whereabouts of their wayward mistresses? I must confess that sometimes I mourn the passing of the age of the master criminal.'

Holmes fumbled within his pockets for some matches and I went over to him with a lighted one of my own. He drew long and gratefully from his old clay pipe.

'Oh come along, my dear fellow, things cannot be as bad as all that,' I said sympathetically, as he slowly arose from his chair.

'You think not? Well then read through this, if you please, while I set about my toilet.' He pulled a brief, crumpled note from the pocket of his dressing-gown and tossed the offending piece of paper disdainfully to the floor. He strode over to the door which he flung open. 'Hot water, Mrs Hudson!' Then, after glancing sheepishly towards me, he added, 'Oh, and bring along some kindling, please.'

My earlier annoyance had, by now, dissipated and I could not help but smile at Holmes's small concession.

I lit a cigarette while I flattened out the note upon the surface of our table. It read as follows:

Dear Mr Holmes
I apologize for having to write to you upon what you will no doubt regard as a trifling matter, but your kindness and discretion were recommended to me by an old friend

11

of mine, *Violet Hunter*, for whom you provided the help and advice that I seek of you now. I am certain that once I have explained, in person, the events that have led to the departure of my mistress from her beloved family home, you will forgive me for bringing my concerns for her well-being to your attention.

If you would grant me a consultation at eleven o'clock tomorrow morning, it would be a blessing.

Yours sincerely
Edith Swinton

While I was reading this through, Mrs Hudson bustled into our room and hurriedly hung the holly and started the fire before Holmes had a chance to change his mind. By the time that he had returned, dressed and revitalized, our room was imbued with a warm and festive glow. He rubbed his hands together contentedly at the sight.

'Thank you, Mrs Hudson.' He smiled as our landlady was taking her leave. 'So, Watson, now that you have read the note, can you reach a conclusion that varies from my own?'

'Well, she does mention Miss Violet Hunter, the helpless young governess whose plight led us upon the affair of the Copper

Beeches. Even though I will concede that this note does not seem to promise much, you have observed on more than one occasion that the most innocuous and mundane-sounding problems have manifested into some of your most challenging and perplexing cases. Surely you will grant her the interview that she seeks?'

'She certainly appears to be a punctual young woman,' Holmes observed quietly, for, as our clock reached the hour of eleven, the doorbell could clearly be heard. Holmes took to his chair by the fire and, by the time that Mrs Hudson had shown our visitor through, Holmes's pipe was fully lit and he was ready to hear Miss Swinton's story. He barely afforded her a single glance as he waved her languidly towards a chair close to his own.

Clearly taken aback by this discourteous greeting, Edith Swinton bravely offered us one of her own.

'Good morning, gentlemen. I trust that you will excuse the brevity of my note, but I am certain that you will soon realize how important it is that I tell you my story in person.'

'That, of course, remains to be seen,' Holmes responded coldly.

I was determined to temper my friend's icy demeanour.

'You will, I am sure, take some coffee before you begin?' I offered.

'That would be most welcome on such a morning.' She smiled gratefully. I called down my request for a tray for three and upon my return I suggested that I take the young lady's coat.

'You will appreciate it all the more when you venture back outside once again,' I explained.

'You are very kind, Dr Watson.'

Holmes arched his eyebrow suspiciously in my direction, although he was probably less aware than I was that the lady had much to commend her to the eye.

She was quite tall and slim and her long elegant neck accentuated this all the more. I judged her to be in her late thirties and I was struck by the rich lustre of her jet-black hair and her flawless skin. Her costume was of neatly trimmed plain grey wool. Holmes cleared his throat and reminded me to pick up my notebook and pencil. He finally turned his attention to our guest.

'Miss Swinton, explain to me, as concisely and exactly as you can, the events and circumstances that have led you to seek my advice upon this matter. You may rely upon the discretion and good intentions of Dr Watson as surely as you can upon my own.'

'I am certain that I can.' She bowed towards me with a brief smile.

'Please be aware,' Holmes continued, 'that apart from the fact that you have spent your entire working life in domestic service and that in the past year or two your hard work and diligence have seen you promoted from the kitchen to become your mistress's housekeeper, I know nothing about you whatsoever. Although . . . ' — Holmes paused for what seemed to be an age and Miss Swinton stole me a questioning glance — 'you do appear to have been somewhat troubled of late and your master is indifferent to your plight. That you live by the coast is obvious from your complexion and I would say that you hail from Kent.'

Miss Swinton had been at the point of putting her coffee cup to her lips when Holmes made these startling observations. She immediately replaced the cup upon her saucer and stared at Holmes in a state of breathless bewilderment.

'Why, Mr Holmes, it is almost as if you know me, although I am certain that we have never met,' she exclaimed. 'Perhaps you have known somebody from within the household?'

'I assure you, Miss Swinton, that I have not,' Holmes replied simply, although by now his manner towards our guest appeared to have thawed somewhat, perhaps from the warmth of the fire, or it may have been something in Miss Swinton's delightful manner.

'Oh, come along, Holmes! How do you know so much about Miss Swinton and her affairs? It really is too bad of you,' I protested.

'You know my method well enough, Watson. After all, you have written about it on more than one occasion; so deduce!' Holmes sank back into his chair and he smiled mischievously as he gripped his pipe stem with his bared, clenched teeth.

I put down my notebook, lit a cigarette and studied Edith Swinton with as much intensity as propriety would allow. Nevertheless I found the process to be both awkward and perplexing.

'Well . . . ' I began uncertainly, but it soon became obvious that my efforts were to be in vain.

'I suppose that you have deduced much from having observed Miss Swinton's hands and there are, indeed, indications of calluses on several fingers of her right hand. Otherwise I can see nothing that might have aided you in your deductions,' I concluded tamely.

I was relieved that my surrender was

greeted with a look of disappointment, rather than the one of self-righteous superiority that Holmes would so often employ.

'Watson, you have seen everything that I have seen, yet you still lack the clarity of vision to interpret them into accurate observations. The calluses would certainly suggest that Miss Swinton has spent many years doing manual labour. Yet the scars of small knife wounds, that you chose to ignore, confirm that she worked in the kitchen, for much of that time.

'However, the wounds are now healed and the calluses soft and pink. Therefore, it seems that she was promoted from this drudgery some while ago. The unfashionable, simple design of her costume would imply that she is still in service but the quality of the wool suggests a position of some authority. The fact that she has done some shopping for the household, tells me that she is now the housekeeper.' He pointed to a bag from Harrison and Webb that lay by her feet.

By now Holmes was leaning forward and clearly warming to his task. His speech became more rapid and his breath a little shorter. He smiled when he observed the look of amazement upon Miss Swinton's face and he paused to re-light his pipe.

'I can also see that Miss Swinton has been

somewhat troubled of late, for she has recently taken to the habit of biting off the tips of her fingernails. I know this is a habit born recently, because her cuticles are still perfectly formed. The rest, I am sure, you can reason for yourself.' Holmes smiled mischievously and expectantly.

'The remainder must surely be speculation,' I murmured, and regretted my chosen words from the moment that I had uttered them.

Holmes immediately leapt to his feet and proceeded to glare down at me, arching his right eyebrow as he did so.

'Watson, you have sorely disappointed me. Have I not told you, time and again, that I never guess?'

'Oh, but really, Holmes, how else could you possibly know, with any certainty, that her master is indifferent to her plight and that she travelled from the Kent coast?' I protested.

'Would Miss Swinton be here today if he were not? Consider the state of the household. His wife has deserted him, under unusual circumstances, and his life has been left in turmoil. Would he allow his valued housekeeper to travel up to Town on a whim were he not otherwise distracted? Even before we hear Miss Swinton's story, I am convinced that the crux of the matter will prove to be the cause of this distraction.' As he finished this last sentence, Holmes appeared to become thoughtful and his voice dropped.

'Well, perhaps, but even you cannot pinpoint Miss Swinton's point of departure with total conviction.'

'We shall see.' Holmes smiled through a curtain of smoke from his pipe, before continuing.

'When you consider the hour of the day, you will concede that Miss Swinton could only have done her shopping on her way to Baker Street from the station. If I remember my Bradshaw correctly, Dungeness is on a small branch line and it is only possible to reach London by changing trains at both Ashford and Appledore. Since Charing Cross is the only London terminus that affords a convenient route that passes Harrison and Webb on the way to Baker Street and also receives the majority of its arrivals from the S.E.R — '

I interrupted Holmes's flow.

'Oh, but, Holmes, that is hardly conclusive evidence!' I protested.

'Perhaps not, but you have surely over-looked one overwhelming proof.' Holmes pointed to the floor at Miss Swinton's feet. 'The return ticket, which fell from Miss Swinton's glove when she reached for her coffee, is clearly marked Dungeness, which as you know is in southern Kent!'

When he saw the look on our faces, Holmes fell back into his chair whilst clapping his hands and laughing uproariously. Miss Swinton and I could not have failed to share the cause of Holmes's amusement and it was a minute or two before our laughter had subsided.

'Well, I must say, I did not think that your deduction would prove to be as simple as that!' I stated.

'Ah, but, Doctor, do not forget that both you and I failed to observe the ticket on the floor.' Somehow Miss Swinton instinctively knew how to cultivate Holmes's inherent flaw of vanity and his manner visibly changed towards her thereafter.

'Nevertheless, Miss Swinton, I still require you to furnish me with the more relevant details of your concern. After all, I am not a mind reader.'

'Of course.' She smiled and I reached for my notebook once again.

'You were correct upon every detail, Mr Holmes. I am indeed in domestic service and I am currently employed as a housekeeper, a position that I have filled for only a short time within the household of Sir Balthazar Dundas, of Dungeness.'

'That is an illustrious household indeed, eh, Holmes?' I asked excitedly.

Sir Balthazar Dundas was one of the rising stars of British politics and his handling of the Prussian Crisis had led many people, within Parliamentary circles, to believe that he would undoubtedly succeed Lord Holdhurst and become the next Foreign Secretary of Great Britain. I glanced across at Holmes as I made this observation, but I could see, from his impassive expression, that the name held no significance for him whatsoever. This was not altogether surprising to me.

I should mention here that Sherlock Holmes had the unique capacity for being able to eliminate from his memory all facts and information that he deemed to be irrelevant to his most singular profession. As a consequence he was as ignorant upon the subjects of, for example, astronomy and affairs of state, as I was upon the qualities of the various forms of cigar ash and their bearing upon criminal investigations.

Nevertheless, it was still inconceivable to me that Holmes did not even have the slightest notion as to the significance of Sir Balthazar Dundas's name. I explained this to him as briefly and patiently as I could and, after acknowledging this with a sharp nod of his head, Holmes motioned to Miss Swinton that she should continue with her story. He leant forward, pressing his forefinger against his pursed lips and closed his eyes tightly in a state of intense and absolute concentration.

'My poor mother and I were abandoned by my feckless father when I was still quite young. He had never been suited to living the life of a family man and he was determined to pursue a life at sea. We subsequently discovered that he had perished when a small merchant ship, on which he had a berth, went down with its entire crew off of the coast of Madeira. My mother had no other family and we were left totally alone and quite penniless.'

'How awful!' I exclaimed, much to the chagrin of Holmes, who now leapt from his seat and strode over to the fireplace for his pipe. Appearing to be unaffected by Holmes's sudden movement, Miss Swinton continued with her story.

'A stroke of good fortune found my mother a position within the Dundas household and they were kind enough to take me in and indulge me until I was of an age when I could be of some use about the house. As you so correctly deduced, Mr Holmes, my first duties were within the kitchen and there I remained until my dear mother was taken from me by tuberculosis.

'She had formed a particularly close bond

with Lady Dundas, who was now determined that I should progress within her large household and, in time, assume my mother's position by her side. I can state, with confidence, that not once did Lady Dundas have cause to doubt the wisdom of her decision and I became her companion as much as I was her housekeeper.

'My close attendance of Lady Dundas, together with my other duties, prevented me from having any time away from the house. However, as a result of the Dundases being such a happy and devoted couple, it was a pleasant household in which to work and, therefore, I did not notice, nor did I feel aggrieved by the deprivation of a life beyond the four walls of their home.'

Miss Swinton paused for a moment so that she could take another sip from her coffee.

Holmes turned towards her earnestly whilst still clutching his pipe.

'However, something then occurred that shattered the tranquil environment that you had hitherto enjoyed?' Holmes asked, speculatively.

Miss Swinton nodded emphatically and repeatedly and gazed up at Holmes through tearful eyes. This was not lost on Holmes.

'Now, now, young lady, once you have furnished me with all of the relevant facts, I assure you that we shall soon put matters to rights,' Holmes promised her gently.

Miss Swinton smiled up at him gratefully and gently wiped her eyes.

'Things were never the same after that awful foreign gentleman paid his first visit to the house during the summer . . . '

Holmes raised his forefinger in front of her so that she should pause in mid-sentence.

'I apologize, but it is absolutely vital that you recount his appearance with as much detail and clarity as you can.' Holmes then waved for her to continue.

'That should not prove to be too difficult, Mr Holmes, for he is a gentleman that I shall not very easily forget. I never did learn his name and Sir Balthazar always interviewed him with the drawing-room door closed firmly behind them. However, on more than one occasion, when their voices were raised, I am certain that the guest spoke with a strong German accent. The gentleman was not particularly tall; however, this was more than adequately compensated for by the strength and power of his . . . ' Miss Swinton cleared her throat and reddened slightly while she searched for the apt and proper descriptive term.

'You mean that he had an unusually strong physique?' I offered.

'Thank you, Doctor, that is precisely what I did mean.' Miss Swinton smiled gratefully towards me as she nodded. Holmes had abandoned his pipe to the mantelpiece, only to replace it with another hastily lit cigarette. He gestured impatiently for her to continue.

'His clothing confirmed his Germanic origins as much as his accent. He wore a pair of tan brogues which were secured with a set of coloured laces, a pair of heavy, green wool trousers and a dark hacking jacket which was matched with a waistcoat and hat. He had a thin red moustache which was shaped in a manner that mirrored his eyebrows and resulted in his every facial movement, even a smile, to resemble a sinister grimace that never failed to cause me to shudder whenever I was unfortunate enough to be in his presence. His flat head was completely bald, save for a thin line that strangely encircled its circumference. His cold, green eyes were like ice; they followed my every movement and seemed to pierce through to my very soul. His bizarre, almost grotesque appearance was set off by — '

'A silver-rimmed monocle over his left eye!'

Miss Swinton's mouth literally gaped open when she heard Holmes's startling pronouncement.

'So you do know the household, after all,'

she said breathlessly.

'Not at all, that was nothing more than a lucky guess, I assure you,' Holmes explained weakly. I was on the point of reminding him that 'he never guessed' when he impatiently waved me to silence.

He returned to his seat, perching himself on its edge, and stared at the young lady with such an intensity that she shuffled to the back of her own, so startled was she by Holmes's behaviour. Her manner suggested that she was no more convinced by Holmes's explanation than I had been.

I was in no doubt that Holmes knew, only too well, the identity of Dundas's frequent and sinister guest and that he had his own good reason for withholding that information from us. I also knew from past and recurring experience that to ask Holmes to expand upon his statement, at this stage, would prove to be a complete waste of time.

'In what way did the visits from this foreign stranger change things within the household?' I asked.

Miss Swinton's voice quivered when she replied, although she was just able to suppress the tears that were threatening to spill from her eyes.

'Oh, Mr Holmes . . . we did not enjoy another peaceful moment from that time onwards! Sir Balthazar was so deeply affected, as a result of their first meeting, that he rarely offered another civil word to anyone. It was Lady Dundas who certainly suffered the most by his vicious tongue. Sir Balthazar would fly into a rage at the slightest provocation and at times he became quite abusive.

'Of course, my mistress attempted to reason with him, but he offered no rational explanation for his extraordinary behaviour and shunned her every approach. It was almost as if he was deliberately forcing her away from him, although it was for reasons that I could not hope to understand.

'After every visit from that awful stranger, Sir Balthazar's behaviour seemed to deteriorate and he offered no attempt at reconciliation even when my mistress threatened to pack her bags and leave him. It was almost as if that was his intention, for it was at this time that he fell into the habit of removing his false teeth at the end of every meal and hurling them in the direction of his horrified wife — '

It was at this point that Holmes held up his hand in front of Miss Swinton and beseeched her to stop. He was so taken aback by her extraordinary words that he was barely able to conceal an amused delight at their bizarre nature. Anything that removed a case from the common plane would entice him in the same way that a rare wine would excite a renowned connoisseur. He lightly fingered his own teeth, as if he needed to confirm the true meaning of Miss Swinton's words.

'Pray tell me how the lady of the house reacted to her husband's outrageous display?' Holmes asked, eventually.

'Very often those awful objects would actually strike her and, with a cry, sometimes of pain and sometimes of surprise and repulsion, she would fly from the table and lock herself in her room. From behind the heavy oak door the sound of her sobbing could frequently be heard. The thing that made Sir Balthazar's behaviour all the more peculiar was the fastidious attention that he normally paid to his dentures. They were made from the very latest and finest porcelain and, once they became tarnished in any way, he would replace them from a seemingly inexhaustible supply. Now, however, he was shattering them at every mealtime and so those tiny cardboard boxes began arriving for him at regular intervals. Each box contained a replacement pair of dentures and he unwrapped each one with an exaggerated anticipation that defied my comprehension. He would then disappear up to the attic.'

'Why on earth would he go to the attic?' I

asked, whilst replenishing Miss Swinton's coffee cup. 'After all, I am sure that it was a large enough establishment for him to be able to avoid his wife without resorting to the top of the house. Of course, I am assuming that this was his reason for taking to such an inhospitable room.'

Miss Swinton sipped slowly and gratefully from her cup before making her reply.

'I am sure that your assumption is a correct one, Doctor, although you should know that he had recently converted the attic into a private observatory from where he could now indulge his newly acquired interest in astronomy. He would spend hours on end up there with his new telescope and the like, leaving us with the instruction that he should not be disturbed under any circumstances.'

'Well, he certainly seems to have taken to his hobby with an admirable conscientiousness,' Holmes commented, while he stared intently at our client. 'Was the observatory installed before or after the initial visit from our sinister stranger?' he then asked.

'It was within a week of that awful . . . awful day,' the young lady lamented.

Holmes eyed me quizzically for a moment. 'That is somewhat suggestive, would you not say, Doctor?' he asked, although he did not await my reply, for he had seen something in Miss Swinton's manner that prompted another question from him.

'Miss Swinton, have you had occasion to visit the attic, for whatever reason, since the installation of the observatory?'

'I only hesitate in mentioning this, Mr Holmes, because I am certain that you will think me quite mad should I do so.'

Holmes dismissed this reservation with a wave of his hand.

'Nevertheless, please explain, in precise detail, everything that you saw while you were up there.'

'Mr Holmes, it is not what I observed that is in question, but it's rather what I heard that I should bring to your attention. Two sounds, in fact, that beggar belief. I ran up the stairs to inform him that his wife was about to depart, with her trunk ready to load, upon the waiting carriage. He dismissed me through the locked door, in such loud and abusive tones that, for a moment or two, I stood rooted to the spot in a state of shock.'

'The bounder!' I exclaimed instinctively, but Holmes silenced me with a glare and an impatient grunt.

Miss Swinton continued unabashed.

'The intense silence that followed was broken by the bewildering sound of Sir Balthazar sobbing to himself in the most heartfelt manner that you could possibly imagine! However, I could not understand why he should have harboured such a profound regret, as it was a tragic occurrence that his own outrageous actions had brought about!'

'Why indeed?' Holmes confirmed, and then urged Miss Swinton to continue. He beckoned her by crooking his fingers as if drawing her closer towards him. 'There was another sound,' he stated simply.

'Oh, yes, Mr Holmes, there was indeed. It was far removed from the other, but equally distinct and more than inexplicable. So much so, in fact, that I began to doubt my own senses and I moved closer to the door in order to confirm my first impression. I had not been mistaken, for undoubtedly and repeatedly from behind the closed observatory door, I could hear the sound of the flapping wings of a gigantic bird.'

Holmes appeared to be exasperated at first, by what he undoubtedly saw as a young woman's fantasy.

'So, it would seem that the observatory has also doubled as an aviary,' he snapped harshly.

'I do not blame you for chiding me for making such a suggestion, for I could scarcely believe it myself when I first heard it.

However, as I turned to climb down the stairs, I happened to glance through the landing window and there, silhouetted against the full white moon, was an enormous sea bird in flight. I am sure that it was a cormorant and it appeared to be heading out towards the sea.'

'You are certain that it was a cormorant?' I asked quietly, not wishing Miss Swinton to think that her every word was to be doubted.

'You forget, Doctor, that I have spent my entire life by the sea and I am quite familiar with the species. I assure you that it was a cormorant,' she stated emphatically.

'That is rather unusual, is it not?' I persisted. 'Surely cormorants make their nests within the sides of cliffs and, as we know, the shoreline around Dungeness is comprised of nothing more than flat, desolate shingle.'

'Perhaps the creature had a long flight ahead of it,' Holmes suggested vacantly. I could tell that his mind was already working out a more logical solution to this mystery, although the nature of this I could only guess at.

'Miss Swinton, as fascinating as this story of yours undoubtedly is, you have not yet furnished me with even one clue that might suggest the location of your sadly departed mistress,' Holmes announced suddenly.

'Oh, but, Mr Holmes, you have surely misinterpreted the reason for my visit to you today. I desire that you help me solve the mystery that has led to Lady Dundas's dramatic departure, not to discover her subsequent destination.

'I received a wire from her only yesterday and she has implored me not to divulge her location to another living soul. However, I am certain that she would allow me one exception were she to know that I intended to consult you upon the matter,' Miss Swinton concluded breathlessly.

Holmes's long, sinewy fingers reached out greedily for the wire and he began to read it with urgent intent.

'It states simply that she has found refuge within the walls of her sister's home near East Grinstead, in Sussex, and does not wish to be contacted until her husband has regained his senses and banished that awful German from their house for good. I would say that your mistress is a very wise and prudent woman, Miss Swinton, and that you could do no better than to attempt to join her there,' Holmes suggested earnestly. He screwed up his eyes in intense concentration and next spoke as if to himself.

'There is a pattern emerging, but I cannot

be sure until I put my enquiries into motion.'

'You think there is the threat of danger, should either Lady Dundas or I return to Dungeness?' the young lady asked quietly.

Holmes did not answer her question directly.

'Miss Swinton, please be good enough to furnish the doctor with the full address of where you might be reached and we will contact you as soon as we have put matters to right.' Holmes sensed her uncertainty as she slowly rose and prepared to leave.

'Matters will come to a head in Dungeness, I assure you. You will be quite safe in East Grinstead.'

'You appear to know far more about the events in the Dundas household than even I do!' she exclaimed. 'Can you not share some of this knowledge with me?'

Holmes smiled briefly and bade her farewell dismissively. I escorted Miss Swinton to the street door, but noticed that Holmes was already filling his cherrywood before we had even left the room!

PART TWO

The Lighthouse

As I stood waiting with Miss Swinton until such time as she was secure aboard a cab, I could not help but notice how the light from a nearby gas-lamp enhanced the warmth and depth of her soft, dark-brown eyes. She appeared uncomfortable once she became aware of my attentions. So I lit up a cigarette and diverted my gaze to the icy winter's sky above us.

A light snow flurry had just begun to fall from the thick white clouds, settling slowly and silently on the surface of the busy thoroughfare in front of us.

'It is lovely when it snows,' she said quietly, once she had followed my gaze. She followed it further when I observed Holmes's stark, hawk-like profile as he smoked his pipe by the large bay window above. He was clearly oblivious to our attention.

'Your friend is a very clever, yet unusually enigmatic gentleman, is he not?' she asked, in a manner that was by no means judgemental.

'He is indeed, but you should have no doubt that he will solve your mystery and restore to you the happiness that you have lost,' I assured her emphatically. At that moment a cab finally answered my summons and I helped Miss Swinton into her seat.

'I thank you both for your great kindness,' she said and placed a special emphasis on the word 'both' so that I would not misinterpret the meaning of her words.

'You shall hear from us soon!' I called out, once the cab was under way, but she did not look back.

I took the stairs to our rooms slowly and thoughtfully, but as I quietly entered the room, Holmes turned suddenly towards me and chastised me without a moment's hesitation.

'Watson, you really should not allow the young lady's undoubted charms to cloud either your vision or your judgement. To me she is merely a client, the first element in a long line of events and deductions that will eventually lead us to the truth. If everything that Miss Swinton has told us is factual in every way, then I assure you that we are about to embark upon a most intriguing, if not unique investigation.'

'Do you have reason to doubt her?' I asked, although without wishing to sound overly defensive of her.

Holmes eyed me quizzically and took a long reflective pull on his pipe before replying.

'You are well aware of my opinion of the

gentler sex, friend Watson. However, on this occasion, I believe that our client is sincere in her interpretation of the events that she has witnessed. As to whether my investigations validate that construer is, of course, an altogether different matter.

'These are very dark waters in which we are about to immerse ourselves; nonetheless I would very much like to hear the opinion of my old friend and trusted associate.' He smiled through a thick plume of smoke and invited me to speak with a dramatic flourish of his left hand.

I lit a cigarette before making my tentative response.

'It is hard for me to speculate, because the chain of events, which Miss Swinton has described to us, is so bizarre and therefore beyond my realm of experience.'

'Do not speculate, Doctor, deduce!' Holmes insisted.

'You have the advantage of me, Holmes,' I protested. 'It is clearly evident, to me, that you have already identified the Dundas's sinister German visitor and, perhaps, even the reasons behind his rendezvous.'

'You are correct in your former assertion, but not the latter,' Holmes conceded. 'I did betray myself, somewhat, with the dramatic declaration that he sported a monocle, although, as you know only too well, I can never pass up the opportunity of causing an effect. However, I should not, even for a moment, have expected you to be duped by my sorry excuse. Oh, he is an Austrian gentleman by the way, not German!'

I found Holmes's manner to be altogether infuriating.

'In heaven's name, Holmes, who is the man?'

Holmes was decidedly unperturbed at my outburst, yet he condescended to identify the Austrian, nonetheless.

'You might recall how, at the outset of the case that you rather unimaginatively entitled 'The Conscientious Constable', Detective Constable Parkes mysteriously disappeared whilst he was conducting a rather long and fruitless surveillance duty?'

'Well, of course I do. Parkes was leading a double — '

'Watson!' Holmes held up his hand in protest. 'It is the object of his surveillance that is of note here, not the case itself. The man that Parkes was observing was none other than Theodore Daxer, the most dangerous and notorious foreign agent now operating on these shores.

'He is more devious than Eduardo Lukas and possesses a far greater propensity for violence than our old friend Oberstein. Believe me, Watson, when I tell you that in these volatile and unstable times, no greater threat to our nation's security exists than the presence of Theodore Daxer.' Holmes concluded this dramatic statement with a flourish of his pipe.

'I do not doubt your word, of course, yet I find it hard to believe that a man such as he is allowed to come and go as he pleases. If, indeed, he poses a threat of a nature that you have described, surely the police, or the government, are entitled to arrest him or even deport him,' I suggested.

'Ah, if only things were that simple, Watson. However we must remember that he has the diplomatic protection of one of the most influential chancelleries in Europe. I refer, of course to the Hapsburgs of the Austro-Hungarian Empire. Until he commits a capital offence he cannot be touched, much less prosecuted. This is regardless of any anguish he might cause within the Dundas household.

'That is not to say, however, that you and I cannot, in our own small way, bring some influence to bear upon the ongoing events. We need to discover the nature of Daxer's hold over Dundas and why he poses such a threat to the safety of his wife.'

Before I could question this last statement of his, Holmes anticipated me and continued breathlessly, 'Oh yes, Watson, I am of little doubt that Dundas's recent abusive treatment of a wife to whom, until recently, he has been so attentive and devoted, has been nothing less than a ruse to drive her from the house and out of harm's way. As hurtful as this may have been to her, Dundas seems to have succeeded without having to betray the reason behind the threat,' Holmes explained, before returning to his seat.

'So that explains why you were so reluctant for Miss Swinton to return to Dungeness. You are implying that she is under the same shadow of threat from Daxer, as is her mistress!' I exclaimed.

'It implies nothing, although I think that it is not unlikely,' Holmes said pensively, while avoiding my gaze. Then he clapped his hands and leapt up to his feet with a sense of real urgency. 'I must be off. If events unfold as I expect them to, there can be no further delay. Call a cab, Mrs Hudson!' His voice rang out suddenly and echoed around the building as he dashed off to his room to obtain his greatcoat and muffler. Upon returning to the room, Holmes hurriedly scribbled a brief wire which he handed to Mrs Hudson with instructions for great urgency.

I managed to attract his attention for just the briefest of moments, before he was able to execute this sudden departure.

'Where shall you go?' I asked. 'I have not heard anything, from either Miss Swinton or yourself, which would indicate to me an obvious destination for your enquiries.'

'Very likely not,' he replied tersely. 'I must admit that one of my ports of call is a purely speculative one. Namely Trinity House, in order that I might consult their register of lighthouses. However, I am more than convinced that a visit to my brother, Mycroft, at his offices in Whitehall, is most certainly long overdue.'

Holmes's manner was so detached, when he made this announcement, that I became convinced that I should have known the reasons behind each of his visits, but I did not.

'So I am to be singularly unemployed once again, it would seem,' I complained.

'No, not at all, old fellow.' Holmes smiled. 'You will be much more valuable to me were you to ensure that your revolver is adequately cleaned and loaded. I would not be at all surprised if there is at least one occasion, during the long night ahead, when it will be called into action.' Holmes's voice dropped as he made this statement and the gravity of the situation was etched into his features.

'So, is it my presence that is required, or merely just that of my revolver?' I asked of him, with a tone of some bitterness in my voice.

'Oh, my dear fellow, I would be honoured to receive your companionship, for there is no one I would rather have by my side on such a night that stretches before us,' Holmes said, somewhat awkwardly.

'Then, of course, you shall have it, Holmes . . . and that of the gun.' I smiled.

'Excellent! Then, in my absence, please be good enough to consult your Bradshaw for the train times to Appledore, and do ensure that we have adequate provisions to see us through till the morning.' Holmes was already halfway down the stairs by the time that he had finished this last sentence. 'I shall be with you at four!' he hollered from the street door. The front door almost shattered into pieces as it slammed behind him.

I set about my simple tasks without a moment's delay. My years of army training ensured that our overnight bag was packed within a few minutes and my Bradshaw recommended a route from Charing Cross to Dungeness, via Ashford and Appledore.

Holmes was as good as his word and he seemed to be pleased with the results of his consultations when he returned to Baker Street at the appointed time. At that moment the butcher's boy burst into our room, brandishing what I had supposed to be the reply to the wire that had been despatched earlier. Holmes tore this open feverishly and then stuffed it into the pocket of his greatcoat.

I would have enquired as to its contents, but I was only too well aware that we needed to make short shrift of our journey to Charing Cross were we not to miss the last train of the day to Appledore. Once I had informed him of this, Holmes spun on his heels and in an instant we were in the cab of Dave 'Gunner' King whose services Holmes had retained in anticipation of this eventuality.

King thundered us through the streets of London at a breathless and breakneck speed so that we arrived upon the platform barely a minute before our train's departure. The cold weather was having its usual effect upon my leg and, as I was equally hampered by the overnight bag, Holmes was already sprawled out upon his seat by the time that I hurled myself aboard. A moment later the guard blew his final whistle and the train lurched forward.

'It was good of you to join me, Doctor!' Holmes laughed.

I had barely recaptured enough breath to

summon up a retort. I merely let the bag drop to the floor before I fell into the seat opposite to Holmes. We had the carriage to ourselves and we did not think twice before lighting up our first pipes of the journey. Initially we smoked in silence, until I became conscious of an air of satisfaction, even triumph, upon my friend's features.

'I do not need to be the world's foremost amateur consulting detective to be able to deduce that you are pleased with your afternoon's work. I should imagine that some of the pieces are beginning to fall together,' I ventured.

Holmes smiled briefly, but then he leant forward and assumed a gravity that caused me to feel for my revolver. He shook his head slowly and deliberately when he spoke.

'Not some of the pieces, Watson, but almost all of them. However, events are unfolding in a way that even I had not foreseen and we may be only just in time to avert a tragedy.'

I was certain that Holmes had absolutely no intention of expanding upon this dramatic statement of his, but I pulled out my notebook and pencil in the hope that I might encourage him to do so.

'I assume that you are referring to the reply of your wire that arrived a moment before our departure,' I suggested.

Holmes looked disdainfully at my writing apparatus but then he responded with an air of reluctance and resignation.

'Well, I suppose we do have some little time on our hands and the contents of that wire are of the greatest moment.'

By now the train was skirting around the southernmost suburbs of our sprawling metropolis. As an early evening dusk began to envelope it, I noticed how much smoke, from even the smallest and most humble of dwellings, was being pumped into the ever darkening sky in an effort by their inhabitants to survive a most bitterly cold evening. Holmes would have been oblivious to these mundane observations of mine and he leant forward eagerly as he passed the wire across for my perusal.

The wire was as brief as it was momentous. To my surprise, its author was none other than the sister of Lady Dundas who briefly confirmed Holmes's worst fears — her sister had never reached her home in East Grinstead.

'I do not understand why you wired her for confirmation in the first place,' I said. 'Did you have cause to doubt the word of Miss Swinton?'

'No, Watson, not at all. However I am well

acquainted with the treacherous ways of Theodore Daxer! If Lady Dundas has fallen into his bloodstained hands, we must act swiftly, for her life will not be worth an hour's purchase, should we not!' Holmes replied dramatically.

'I can see now the need for some urgency. However, you were already hell bent on making this journey before the arrival of the wire. I presume that you were acting upon information that you received from Trinity House and from your brother Mycroft.'

Holmes nodded emphatically by way of a reply, and then pulled long and contentedly upon his pipe, as if he was savouring its delights for the first time, before continuing with his response.

'You might well recall how, on no less than three separate occasions, my brother Mycroft has called upon our services. Most recently, of course, was the affair of Baron Maupen-tuis, an escapade that very nearly cost me my life at the hands of the late Professor Moriarty. Each one of those adventures, I believe, eventually found their way into your lamentably colourful journals and provided me with their own set of unique challenges.

'In any event, I felt that it was now time for Mycroft to reciprocate and I lost no time in making my way to his offices in Whitehall. I was in little doubt that I would find him at his desk, even though I was to be unannounced, as his daily schedule is more regimented than that of a Bradshaw and infinitely more reliable. I was not to be disappointed and, since his desk was clear, I learnt that I was to receive his full and undivided attention.

'Although it is true to say that time has not dealt kindly with my brother, I am glad to report that it has not yet diminished his capacity for the retention and the analysis of facts and information that is still greater than that of any man living. Of course, were it not for his complete lack of energy and ambition, his reputation would surpass even that of your celebrated friend.

'Mycroft immediately sent down for a decanter of his best port wine and two of his favourite hand-rolled cigars. Once we had drunk and smoked in silence for a while, my brother put me right about a good many things. I had gone to seek his advice with the preconceived notion that Daxer's hold over Dundas had its roots in Dundas's handling of the Prussian Crisis, the event that precipitated his meteoric rise to political imminence.

'As you are doubtless aware, the House of Hapsburg was involved in that potentially devastating diplomatic crisis. So, naturally enough, Daxer's interest would have been immediately aroused. Therefore, it would not have been beyond the bounds of reason to surmise that the government, which he served, would require Daxer to search for any weakness in their diplomatic enemy.

'I explained my concerns to Mycroft in the hope that he might describe to me the nature of any potentially sensitive material which Daxer might coerce Dundas into providing him, given the right kind of persuasion. The wiles and deceit of international diplomacy have had an unfortunate effect upon the behaviour of many a fine public servant. Well, Watson, I can tell you now that my assertion could not have been further from the truth!'

At this juncture Holmes leant back in his seat once more so that he could fully observe the effect of these last words of his. He was not to be disappointed. I stopped writing in my notebook immediately and eyed my friend incredulously.

'Oh yes, Watson, although that is not to say that Daxer did not have a hold over our future Foreign Secretary. Its nature, however, would never have occurred to a cold-hearted automaton, like me, simply because Dundas's devotion to his wife defies all reasonable logic. Of course, you would appreciate this far more readily than I ever could and Daxer immediately recognized the potential of exploiting what he perceived as Dundas's only weakness: his fear of a very real threat to the well-being of his wife.

'Daxer had sought every other means of persuading Dundas to betray his government and his country. At each step, however, he had been thwarted by both Dundas's loyalty and integrity. His career has progressed without the slightest blemish appearing on his character and there were no shadows hanging over any of his actions or decisions. He remains a veritable paragon of political virtue.'

Holmes paused for a moment and he appeared to be lost in deep thought as he slowly and deliberately relit his pipe. I used this opportunity to voice a burning question of my own.

'Holmes, I fail to see how your brother came to possess such a profound understanding of this affair. After all, Dundas had, evidently, gone to great lengths to conceal his treachery. The only way Mycroft could have possibly found out about it, would have been if Dundas had gone to Whitehall and spoken to Mycroft himself. Now he was hardly likely to do that!' I protested, once I realized that Holmes had no intention of responding to my question.

'There is precious little that occurs in

Whitehall that escapes my brother's attention, I can assure you, Watson,' Holmes replied languidly. 'However, despite your scepticism, Dundas did go to Mycroft to seek his advice upon the matter. He had nothing to hide and desired to do his best by his country. They decided to play a most dangerous game by promising to supply Daxer with the documents that he had demanded from Dundas.' Holmes held up his hand to prevent me from voicing my inevitable protest, before he continued with his explanation.

'Mycroft would not divulge concise details of these documents, even to me. He assured me, however, that the contents of the papers that they had supplied Daxer were fabrications and would grant our enemies no advantage whatsoever. Daxer would not be aware of this however, until the final message was sent to him. This has been deliberately withheld from him and is now a day overdue. That is why we can be so certain that matters will come to a head tonight.'

'In heaven's name, Holmes, why were you not asked to intervene until now?' I asked incredulously.

'I was on the point of asking Mycroft that very same question when he dropped a draft wire onto the desk in front of me. He could not be sure that I would be needed until

Mycroft's observers became aware of a boat, moored off the coast at Dungeness, which they deduced had been sent to carry Daxer to safety after his night's work.

'Besides, Dundas wanted to involve as few people as possible in case it jeopardized the safety of his wife. You see, they only became aware of her abduction at the same time as we have done. We can only guess at the form of revenge that Daxer now seeks to invoke and therefore, we must be prepared for every eventuality. Our role is to keep Dundas's house under surveillance and the Kent police will only act upon our signal.'

With that Holmes sank back into his seat, as if the effort of imparting so much information had completely exhausted him. Then slowly and inexplicably, Holmes began to close his eyes.

'But, Holmes,' I protested, 'this is hardly the time to fall asleep! You have yet to say a word of your visit to Trinity House.'

Holmes half opened his eyes and raised his left eyebrow in an irritable arch.

'I will commend just this to you, Watson. Trinity House is the veritable institution where they store the national register of lighthouses. Remember, there are no cliffs near Dungeness. Now I suggest that you take some rest yourself, for we have a long and treacherous night's work ahead of us and Ashford is only an hour away.'

With those final, enigmatic and exasperating words, Holmes closed his eyes once more and he would not open them again until we reached our first change of train, at Ashford. Unfortunately, I could not follow Holmes's lead. I found that sleep was impossible as I tried to make some sense out of the complex information that Holmes had furnished me with.

Holmes seemed to consider that his visit to Trinity House and the absence of any cliffs in Dungeness were in some way connected. I could see no connection myself, yet it reminded me of Miss Swinton and her reference to a gigantic cormorant making its flight away from the Dundas's observatory.

Of course, there was also the burning question of how Mycroft could entertain the thought of Daxer retaining his liberty for so long, in the light of his posing so great a threat to the security of our country and the safe return of Lady Dundas. Where could she possibly be now?

I shook my head violently, as if that very action was going to activate a logical chain of events in my brain. Of course, it would not and I merely lit a cigarette and peered through our mist-tinted window at the icy, shimmering landscape that our train was forging its way through.

I glanced admiringly at my friend, as he was sprawled motionless across his seat and could only marvel at his ability to remain so calm in the face of the adventure still to come. I pulled my revolver from my jacket pocket and reassured myself, yet again, that it was loaded and ready for its deadly use.

Another cigarette, or two, found us pulling up at the platform at Ashford. I shook Holmes violently by the shoulder, but the guard was already blowing his whistle by the time that we had bundled ourselves out of the train, so deep had been Holmes's slumber. If we had missed our connection to Appledore all, indeed, would have been lost.

The stretch from Ashford to Appledore, although considerably shorter than our earlier journey, was a slow and laborious affair. The track was as old as our carriage and the discomfort of being constantly buffeted around was only tempered by the intense cold that our leaky old car was allowing in. I dreaded to think what the final leg of our journey, along the seldom used single track to Dungeness, was going to be like.

As it transpired, my fears proved to be unfounded. The ancient single gauge track was soundless and smooth so that we pulled up at the platform in Dungeness in virtual silence. This was partly true because my friend maintained his reticence in offering me any further information. He did issue me with a grave warning, however, once we had procured a small trap and mare for the final phase of our journey to the home of the Dundases.

'Be aware, Watson, that Dundas has placed himself in great danger. He has been deliberately withholding a vital piece of information without which the remainder has been rendered as completely useless! Tonight, unless I have missed my mark, Theodore Daxer is preparing to exact a fearsome vengeance. I trust that you can now see why it is absolutely imperative that we are on hand to prevent this from happening. Of course, it also gives us the opportunity of catching Theodore Daxer red-handed into the bargain!'

With that, Holmes gee'd up the mare with a single and gentle stroke from his whip and we proceeded along the muddy, stone-strewn dirt track towards our final destination. We had taken directions from an elderly station master and, after half an hour had passed in like fashion, we pulled up and tethered the trap at a considerable, though discreet, distance from the house.

We were both grateful for our canes as we proceeded precariously on foot. There was a hard frost and we had only the partial illumination from the moon to guide us. However, we finally reached the outer perimeter of the Dundas estate and managed to scramble our way over a small, vine-infested, brick wall, to gain access to the main grounds. We skirted the house, which was an unusual, mock-Tudor pile, as we searched for an outbuilding, that would afford us with a comprehensive view of the imposing residence.

So it was that we found ourselves in the tiny stable that afforded us with a perfect view, across a broad expanse of lawn, of the home of Sir Balthazar Dundas.

By the time that I had concluded my long, though largely unenlightening, chain of thought, the effect of Holmes's generous dose of Cognac had long worn off and I had assumed my former position by the window once more. Holmes was seated in the corner of the room, draped in his blanket; however, every few minutes, he was emitting short grunts of impatience, as his frustration increased.

I was on the point of suggesting that we should abandon our fruitless and brutal vigil, when I saw something that caused me to question whether the intense cold had now had an adverse effect upon my senses. I could scarcely believe my eyes as a long, grey plume of smoke began billowing out from one of the uppermost windows. This was followed by a deadly arrow of orange and red flame that began licking at the rooftop and reaching towards the heavens. I immediately called this dreadful vision to Holmes's attention.

'Hurry, Watson, it would seem that Daxer is covering his tracks with a far more ruthless efficiency that even I could have imagined!'

In an instant we vacated our tiny shelter and, ignoring the intensifying snowstorm, we tore across the lawn to raise the alarm at the house. To my great surprise, we were greeted at the front door by three police constables, who immediately informed us that the household had been roused and were sheltering in one of the outhouses.

I soon realized that Holmes did not seem to be in the least bit taken aback by the presence of the officers and I saw him giving them instructions as I went to check for injuries amongst the household. I was pleased to note that everybody had escaped unscathed; however, there was no sign of Dundas or his wife.

'Come along, Watson! There really is no time to lose!' Holmes called to me as I returned to the front of the house. I had no time even to draw breath, before Holmes bundled me towards the path that led us back to the trap and mare.

PART THREE

The Trained Cormorant

Once we were safely aboard our precarious transport, I found that I could no longer contain myself.

'Really, Holmes, on this occasion you have surely surpassed yourself. Your shabby treatment of me displays a wanton lack of respect that I surely don't deserve!' I complained. 'After all, I have been your man throughout every step of the journey and yet you seem to have expected those constables to be there, almost as if you had arranged it. Where in heaven's name is Dundas, or, indeed, Daxer himself?'

'It really is too bad of me, Watson, and I do owe you a thousand apologies. I will clarify the situation to you in the little time available to us before we reach the Old Lighthouse of Dungeness. Mercifully we have a full hour before high tide by which time we will surely have our man!'

I lit up a cigarette while Holmes gathered his thoughts and I calmed myself in anticipation of his explanations.

'There really is very little for me to add to the earlier summary of events. Dundas's reason for driving his wife away from him was absolutely genuine, for Daxer posed a very real danger to all those who lived within the house. I anticipated that Daxer would seek his revenge tonight, because last night was the first time that the cormorant had not returned safely to him with its vital message. Hence the presence of the constables, which you so correctly surmised, was by my arrangement.'

I now interrupted Holmes for a moment, as I sensed that we were now closing in upon our quarry.

'Surely you had not anticipated the fire and the threat that it poses to Dundas's safety?' I asked hurriedly.

'No, indeed, for even I could not have expected that kind of a reaction from Daxer. This act of vengeful destruction is unique in my experience. Yet every precaution has been taken and the fire engine has already been sent for. As for the whereabouts of Dundas and his wife . . . well, I sincerely hope that the answer lies within the Old Lighthouse.'

It was only now, when we were so close to our journey's end that I realized that a trained cormorant had been Daxer's means of receiving those messages from Dundas. The Old Lighthouse was Daxer's hideaway and Mycroft had been sending the false information to Dundas concealed within the boxes of false teeth.

I was on the point of declaring my sudden enlightenment to Holmes when he raised his hand in front of my mouth and pulled the mare to a halt.

'We shall have to proceed on foot from this point, I am afraid,' Holmes whispered. 'Our approach must be in complete silence if we are to successfully spring our trap. Mark you well, Watson, we shall only have one attempt at apprehending a most dangerous criminal, for at high tide he will surely be gone for good.'

We proceeded as stealthily as we could, but the freezing snow that was crunching beneath our boots, somewhat hindered our desire for absolute silence. We kept very low as we progressed, and in the distance I could hear the sound of the ocean's waves rushing over the shingle of the remote and desolate beach. Surely high tide was not long off and I found myself clutching the handle of my revolver.

Slowly the outline of the shape of a lighthouse began to emerge through the curtain of the swirling snow and it was certainly now no more than a hundred yards away from us. I could not help but wonder at the value of a lighthouse so far removed from the actual shore. Then again, Holmes had referred to it as the Old Lighthouse so presumably there was a newer and more useful one closer to the actual coastline.

As we drew ever closer, the shape of the lighthouse became still more distinct. The snowfall had begun to ease somewhat, and I was certain that I could see the shadows of two people moving at the base of the lighthouse. I was so startled by this apparition that I gripped Holmes firmly at the shoulder and pointed urgently towards the moving shapes.

'Do not trouble yourself, Watson,' Holmes whispered, 'for that is surely Detective Sergeant Spencer Routledge, a most able and talented protégé of Stanley Hopkins, together with two of his best men. He has been as good as his word. Now, we must crouch even lower, for see how one of Routledge's officers is peering up towards the top of the staircase. He shakes his head so I think we still have a little time. At his signal we shall rush for the stairs. Are you ready, old fellow?'

At the mention of Hopkins's name I immediately felt both relieved and impressed. I felt relieved because, up to that very moment, I had convinced myself that the shadowy shapes had been some of Daxer's accomplices. Impressed, because Inspector Stanley Hopkins had been involved in no fewer than seven of our previous cases and on each occasion he had conducted himself most admirably.

Therefore I did not hesitate before making my reply. 'Of course I am,' I said, as Holmes offered me one of his cigarettes. I accepted this eagerly and, of necessity, we smoked in silence.

In the distance I thought that I could hear someone calling from the direction of the sea. Then, almost lost within the glare of the rotating light of the functioning lighthouse, I could make out a response to the call, by way of a signal from a large lantern at the top of the lighthouse nearest to us.

This was surely the moment for Holmes and I to make our move. Undoubtedly Daxer would be down the stairs in an instant, ready to join his comrades in a boat positioned just offshore. The significance of the signal was not lost on Holmes either. He gripped me by the shoulder as he began to edge ever closer to Daxer's lair. I followed his lead, although there was now considerably more urgency in our progress.

As we approached the staircase, Holmes signalled for Routledge's men to disperse, although the young sergeant was to remain in close attendance. By now the revolver was gripped firmly in my hand and I followed

Holmes closely as he began to creep slowly up the stairs. There was absolute silence upon the upper platform and, just for a fleeting moment, I feared that somehow the Austrian had managed to elude us. A second later, however, another signal to the boat reflected down the stairs and we heard a pair of boots turn suddenly and make their way urgently towards our position.

Evidently our stealth had sorely missed the mark, for the very first thing that we saw, upon gaining the upper platform, was the barrel of a German Luger being thrust determinedly against the side of Holmes's head.

'Ah, so they have sent their very best!' Daxer declared.

'You know me then?' Holmes replied.

'I would be a poor professional, indeed, if I were not familiar with the illustrious, though clumsy Sherlock Holmes!' Daxer cackled unpleasantly, as he spat out these words and placed his gun even closer to Holmes's head.

'Now come along, Dr Watson, you must throw your gun down immediately, before I splatter your colleague's fine brain about this magnificent old lighthouse. Be quick, please, for I do not wish to miss my boat,' Daxer ordered viciously.

'Do not do it, Watson!' Holmes called out.

'The only crime for which Herr Daxer does not have full immunity is murder. He has no intention of killing me, I can assure you.'

'Do not be so sure, Holmes, for I have a boat, just a few yards away, waiting to carry me back to the safety of my homeland,' Daxer responded, although with a little less certainty in his voice. 'Now drop your gun at once and the two of you must climb slowly to join me up here.'

My dilemma was obvious to the two of them. It was not in my nature to disobey Holmes; however, there was a certain desperation in Daxer's voice that caused me to fear for Holmes's life. I let go of my trusty revolver and felt despair as I heard the heavy metal echo around the building as it clattered to the bottom of the stairs.

Holmes glanced down towards me before ascending to the platform; however, I was surprised to see that there was neither anger nor disappointment in his eyes. I shuffled slowly up the stairs to join them and the three of us stood face to face close to the derelict old beacon in the centre of the room.

I realized at once that Miss Swinton's description of Daxer had been a precise and accurate one. He was a little shorter than I had imagined him to be and somewhat thicker about the girth, but his appearance was every bit as vicious and threatening as she had described him. His guttural voice and his strong accent only increased the man's inherent menace, as did his cold, sinister eyes.

'It is so good of you both to join me.' He smirked sadistically and, as he spoke, he threw me a length of thick, coarse rope.

'Now, Dr Watson, it is my desire that you take your colleague's wrists and bind them as tightly as you can to the rail that surrounds the beacon over here. Be careful, mind you, for if I am not satisfied with the security of your knots I will shoot him without a moment's hesitation.' His thin lips separated into a repugnant smile as he gave out his order and he pulled back the hammer of his gun to increase the threat.

'This is intolerable!' I protested, as I bent down to carry out Daxer's bidding.

'Perhaps it is, Doctor, but the alternative would be far worse, I assure you,' Daxer goaded.

Holmes smiled up at me ironically as he positioned his wrists in the required position.

'Please ensure that the knots are fast and true, Doctor, for you would not relish the alternative option, of that I am certain,' he said.

'You do not have to worry about that,' I said defiantly, while glaring towards our captor. Once I had completed the task, Daxer inspected my work. Obviously he was satisfied with my knots, for he immediately turned his gun away from Holmes's head. Then, to my dismay and astonishment, he turned the weapon towards me!

'Sadly, Doctor, there is no one left to tie your knots. Therefore I have devised a more rudimentary means of preventing you from pursuing me. Simply put, once I have despatched my final signal to the waiting boat I fully intend to shoot out both of your kneecaps.'

He said this with an unnaturally sadistic relish and even while he opened and closed the flap to his lantern in the direction of the sea, neither his eyes nor his gun left me for a second.

He completed the signal and turned his attention towards me once more.

'All is now in readiness, you will be glad to hear.' Daxer smiled malevolently.

'Before you pull the trigger, there is just the one thing that I need you to clarify for me!' Holmes suddenly shouted out.

'Now is hardly the time, Herr Holmes,' Daxer remarked quickly.

'Nevertheless, surely a minute or two will make little difference to you as the tide has not yet fully turned in your favour. Besides, as you can see, I can no longer pose a threat to you.' Holmes made an attempt to raise his hands in vain, to demonstrate how impotent he now was.

'This is true; so, quickly now, how can I further enlighten you?' Daxer could not suppress a manic smile as he contemplated the sense of power this situation was giving him.

'I just need to know how you managed to dispose of Jethro Styles, the former occupant of this lighthouse and the man who trained the cormorant that brought you the messages from Dundas.'

Daxer studied Holmes thoughtfully and for a moment the glint behind the monocle seemed to fade.

'You have certainly invested much time in looking into my affairs. Oh, but Mr Holmes you do disappoint me. Everybody knows that Styles slipped upon the stairway and broke his neck in the fall. A tragedy really, for he was most gifted at the training of birds.' By the time Daxer had finished speaking, the glint had returned, as had his malicious smile.

'That, of course, is the official line,' Holmes responded. 'However, it was common knowledge that Styles had lived in this lighthouse for the best part of thirty years and had probably been up and down those steps a thousand times. You cannot expect me to believe that a man of your dubious reputation had nothing to do with his death.'

By this time Holmes had so distracted him that Daxer's revolver was now hanging loosely by his side as he turned to face him.

'The sense of justice and fair play, which are so dear to you British, never fails to amuse me,' Daxer smirked. 'You know that within a few moments I will be on a boat that will carry me away from these accursed shores for ever and yet you have to know the truth no matter how redundant it may be.

'It does not matter now, of course, but it was merely a trifling matter of loosening a few nuts and bolts on the uppermost hand rail that ensured the premature demise of Jethro Styles. Do you know what? Despite the harsh winds and the slippery stones, the fellow still would not fall of his own accord. It was a good job that I was around to provide him with a helping hand.' The dastardly fellow could hardly contain himself as he recounted the death of the unfortunate lighthouse-keeper.

'You might regard it as a trifling matter, Herr Daxer, yet it is nothing less than murder, the only crime for which you do not have diplomatic immunity. Did you catch all of that, Detective Sergeant Routledge?'

Holmes shouted out suddenly.

'I heard every last damnable word that he said, Mr Holmes, loud and clear.' The response did not come from the base of the stairs, where we had last seen him, for Routledge was now standing immediately behind my right shoulder and he was holding my gun.

As Daxer turned in horror to face the young police officer, I brought the handle of my cane crashing down upon Daxer's hand and sent the Luger clattering down on to the grey stone floor. An instant later, Routledge and his men had the vile Austrian securely fastened in a set of handcuffs and Daxer stood there quivering with rage while a torrent of German expletives exploded out from his contemptible mouth.

'Well done, Watson!' Holmes called out. 'Now, would you do me the very great favour of untying your most excellent knots?'

I lost no time in releasing my friend and an instant later Holmes was back onto his feet and he glared down at our captive.

'If your men are quick, Routledge, you might yet add Daxer's accomplices to your bag. I will send them a signal, as Daxer, telling them that they should remain where they are, for I have observed that they have only been using a simple Morse code,'

Holmes explained, and Routledge despatched his men without a second's delay.

To our surprise and, despite everything that had just transpired, Daxer still seemed to be able to emit one of his hideous, guttural laughs.

'Oh, you have completed the thing very well, Mr Holmes, but you should enjoy the moment while you may. I know that my people will not rest for a single minute until they have avenged me. Your life will not be worth a single Austrian schilling from this moment on, I can assure you,' Daxer threatened.

This time it was Holmes who felt compelled to laugh.

'Many people have said as much to me before and yet here I remain. Although my life may be only worth a schilling, I can assure you that, by the time British justice has dealt with you, Herr Daxer, it is a far higher valuation than I would attach to yours!'

This time Daxer could not summon a suitable response.

'You may now remove this person, Detective Routledge, and may I say that I now fully understand why Hopkins holds you in such a high regard. You have quite a prize in your hands with which to further enhance your growing reputation,' Holmes smiled.

'That is very kind of you, Mr Holmes. I can assure you that there is not a single man who knew Jethro Styles, who will not cheer on the day that his murderer keeps his appointment with the hangman. Yet surely the prize is yours,' Routledge offered bashfully.

Holmes waved this aside with aplomb.

'Not at all,' Holmes replied, as Routledge nudged Daxer towards the top of the stairs. All the way down, we could hear Daxer's voice echoing back up to us.

'One schilling Mr Holmes ... one schilling!'

'I must congratulate you for some excellent work with your cane, Watson,' Holmes said, as he slapped me upon the shoulder. However, I was not to be so easily placated.

'You have used and manipulated me, Holmes, and this is not the first or only time! I sincerely believed that our lives were under serious threat, yet all along you had arranged with Routledge a means of manoeuvring Daxer into making a full confession to murder. I feel that I deserve better treatment at your hands.'

Holmes could see at once that mine was a serious complaint and not one that he could laugh away.

'Oh I do apologize, my dear fellow, yet I did not manipulate you. I relied upon one thing alone. I knew that your affection for me would compel you to throw away your faithful revolver, regardless of how painful that action might be for you. Please understand that I had to provide Daxer with a false sense of security by allowing him to believe that he had control of the situation. How else would he feel confident enough to reveal himself as the murderer of Jethro Styles?'

'Well, I am glad that I was able to oblige,' I replied with some bitterness.

It was at this point that I became aware of somebody else standing between Routledge and his constables. It took me very little time to realize that this gentleman was none other than Sir Balthazar Dundas himself. I recognized his description from the papers at once, as he stood at an overbearing six and a half feet and sported a magnificent jet-black moustache.

He stepped forward and presented his hand to Holmes with as much dignity as his emotions would allow. Holmes received his hand warmly and immediately apologized for his short-sightedness in allowing the destruction of Dundas's home.

'You have performed a great service on behalf of your country, by removing the threat of the vermin that is Theodore Daxer,'

Dundas declared, by way of dismissing Holmes's apology as unnecessary. 'At least you had the foresight to ensure that the house was evacuated prior to Daxer's onslaught, without which I should not be standing here now.'

Holmes bowed in acknowledgement of, what he would always view as, a tainted compliment.

'My house can always be rebuilt and my property restored to me,' Dundas continued. 'Yet I would gladly dispense with the lot if you could reunite me with my beloved wife. What has that blackguard done with her? I almost died when I learnt that she did not reach her sister's house in East Grinstead. I can assure you that I have feared the worst ever since.' Dundas could hardly contain himself while he made this plea of Holmes.

'Well, let me see if I can put this matter to rights.' Holmes could barely suppress a smile as he led us all back down the stairs to the base of the lighthouse. We followed him round to the far side of the building where we found a small trap door that, in former times, had been used to store supplies. The twin doors were secured by a large padlock and, with a gesture of his hand, Holmes invited me to put my revolver to good use.

I was careful to ensure that my bullet only

struck upon metal and with a single shot I was able to take out the lock. Dundas hurriedly pulled the doors apart, for by now we all understood the meaning behind Holmes's diversion. Dundas was on the point of descending the small set of stairs, when Holmes restrained him with a hand on his shoulder.

'I think it best that the good doctor goes down first,' Holmes stated ominously, for we could not be certain of the condition in which we would find Lady Dundas. I followed Holmes's instruction without a moment's hesitation and Routledge handed me a lantern with which I could guide my short, but precarious descent.

The dank, cold room had been redundant for many a year and was completely empty save for a small wooden chair in its far corner. It was with intense relief that I realized that the shape upon it was moving! I raced over to release the lady's bindings and remove the muffler that had been preventing her from crying out.

Even in her present sorry state I could see that Lady Dundas was, indeed, a woman of rare beauty. Her rich black hair was in complete disarray and her clothing was torn and covered in the filth of this cold and ancient basement. Yet the light from her eyes shone out despite the long days of dark captivity that she had endured.

Once my brief examination had revealed that she was in no need of medical attention I summoned her husband, that he might assist me in bringing her up the stairs. It was gratifying to see the couple embrace when we had reached ground level once more, and the joy they shared at their safe reunion. I could sense that this display left Holmes feeling uncomfortable and he turned away whilst nervously clearing his throat.

His discomfort was not helped by Lady Dundas repeatedly thanking him for bringing them back together and he smiled briefly before lighting a cigarette. It was decided that the Dundases would join Miss Swinton in East Grinstead for the time being, and Routledge agreed to take their statements after Christmas.

As they were turning away to begin their long journey I could not help but ask Sir Balthazar one last question.

'Was there a significance attached to your behaviour with your false teeth, or was it merely just a fad?'

'It was decided that Mycroft Holmes would send me the information, intended for Daxer, within the boxes in which they were delivered. By continually shattering them I ensured that the arrival of a new pair would not arouse suspicion.

'Of course, my dear wife would never have left me under normal circumstances, and I hurled the teeth in her direction reluctantly, in the hope that I would drive her away from me and to safety. I can only hope that, in time, she can learn to forgive my dreadful behaviour throughout those dark days.'

Lady Dundas hooked her arm through his as her answer and they walked slowly away through a thin wall of fluttering snow.

Once they were gone and Holmes had assured Routledge of his full co-operation upon matters reaching the courts, we turned away from the Old Lighthouse of Dungeness, a building that had now assumed a dark and ominous persona, and began to trudge back towards our trap.

'Holmes, how did you know that Lady Dundas had been incarcerated here, at the lighthouse?' I asked.

Holmes turned towards me and smiled.

'Because, friend Watson, I knew that she could be nowhere else. Ha!' he exclaimed, somewhat unsatisfactorily. With that he turned away and began to walk rapidly away from me. He then called back over his shoulder, 'now, come along, Watson. There is a long journey ahead of us and the weather has not become any less harsh. We must try not to further spoil Mrs Hudson's yuletide preparations.'

I could not have agreed more and I felt strangely elated that I had made the decision to cut short my visit to Goole.

2

THE ABERNETTY MYSTERY

' . . . *You will remember, Watson, how the dreadful business of the Abernetty family was first brought to my notice by the depth which the parsley had sunk into the butter upon a hot day.'*

(*The Six Napoleons* by A. Conan Doyle)

PART ONE

Reunions

'It would seem, Watson, that I might have seriously erred these many years!'

'You, Holmes, of all people, surely not?'

On so many occasions throughout our long association, I had been left aghast at Holmes's apparent lack of humility, bordering at times on the arrogant, that I now found it impossible to react to this astonishing statement of his without a touch of condescension and sarcasm in my voice. This was not lost on my friend, who glanced suspiciously towards me, before responding.

'Watson, despite your feigned display of disbelief, this occurrence is not as uncommon as you would have your long-suffering readers believe.'

I could not fathom as to what line of thought might have manifested itself into Holmes's unexpected statement. The past three months had seen his career and reputation climb to unprecedented heights, and this auspicious period had culminated in the successful conclusion of the problem of the Egyptian Gargoyle. The outcome of this foray into international affairs will have to remain shrouded in mystery until such time as Holmes's brother Mycroft deems it appropriate for me to release the details into the public domain. However, despite this indubitable triumph of his, here was Sherlock Holmes admitting to error.

'It is not a professional oversight to which I refer, for as you are no doubt aware, I have been enjoying considerable success of late in that area. Nonetheless, a long held notion of mine does appear to have been ill advised, at best.'

We had paused, for a moment, as we were sauntering along the Charing Cross Road, on our way to Holmes's favourite antiquarian bookshop. Holmes turned towards me, smiling mischievously and trying to gauge as to whether he had succeeded in attracting my attention. It only took a second or two for him to realize that he had done so.

'In heaven's name, Holmes, I am sure that I have no idea as to what you could possibly mean by this,' I complained.

It was unusual to find Holmes bedecked in anything other than his customary black frock coat. But on such a fine late-summer's morning he had decided to bring out a light-coloured linen suit and a boater to match. As I watched him slowly light a cigarette I realized that this was the most relaxed that I had seen him in many months.

'As you have noted on many occasions, I have always pushed myself to extreme physical limits whenever I am actively engaged on a case, with no apparent regard for my own well-being. I am undoubtedly blessed with a constitution that is able to withstand these rigours and yet I too easily forget that I also extend my mental faculties to the very edge of their capacity.

'Surely the human mind is as much constituted of muscle and tissue matter as is the humble thigh or foot and is therefore also capable of becoming similarly fatigued. As a man of medicine I am certain that you will recognize the need to allow the brain some respite. So, acting upon these considerations, I have decided to take a holiday.'

I could not fault a word of his reasoning and I certainly welcomed the conclusions that he had reached. Yet, as I heard those words from my friend's mouth, I found myself unable to suppress a riotous laugh of surprise.

'Well, I must say, Holmes, I would never have expected to hear such a proposal from you, of all people,' I said, once I had calmed myself somewhat.

'I am certainly glad that my little idea has induced so much merriment in you,' he responded sharply, obviously feeling put out by my spontaneous reaction.

'I am most pleased by your surprising decision. But have you not always said that you are loath to leave the capital lest the criminal classes are left to their own devices?'

'Since the demise of Moriarty, and as a result of these last few fulfilling months, I feel confident that the regular police force is more than capable of containing them. Well . . . for a short while at least,' he added thoughtfully.

'But where shall you go?'

By this time we had reached our destination and I waited a full twenty minutes while Holmes perused the latest additions to the book-seller's stock, before I received my reply. Holmes emerged empty handed and he shook his head disconsolately.

'There is nothing of interest or of note,' he grumbled.

As we made our leisurely return to Baker Street, Holmes outlined the plans for his trip.

'Daniel Collier, his new wife and his sister, Charlotte, have all recently made their long awaited return from their mission in Matabeleland. I received a letter from them this very morning, inviting us to spend a week or two with them at their new villa near the Kent coast. I accepted without hesitation.'

For those of you who are, as yet, unfamiliar

with the name, Daniel Collier was the young man who introduced us to the mystery of the 'Giant Rat of Sumatra', through the letters of his tragic father, Sir Michael.

'When will you depart?' I asked.

'I had hoped that you might join me,' Holmes suggested tentatively. 'There is said to be some excellent fishing to be had in the vicinity.'

I was certain, by now, that Holmes had already accepted the invitation on my behalf, but I refused to make this situation any easier for him. While it is true to say that the thought of reacquainting myself with young Collier and the opportunity of meeting his family was a very appealing one, far too often during our association, Holmes had presumed upon my compliance with all of his plans.

'Really, Holmes, it is bad enough that you take me for granted when you need my assistance upon a professional matter, now, however, you have taken it upon yourself to organize my social arrangements also! This presumption of yours is truly beyond the pale,' I protested.

Holmes was visibly taken aback by my outburst.

'Oh my dear fellow.' He smiled meekly. 'I would never so presume, but rather sincerely hoped that my plans would prove to be agreeable to you. Nevertheless, upon my arrival at the Colliers' villa, I will explain that you are somewhat pressed at your surgery of late. I am certain that they will accept this without taking exception to your absence.'

'Well, my surgery has been rather quiet in recent weeks, and the opportunity to reacquaint myself with young Daniel Collier is certainly very inviting. It would be nice to meet his family and, if I were to accompany you, at least I could be certain that your holiday is not interrupted by any of those untimely problems that always seem to present themselves.' My annoyance at Holmes's presumptive response to Collier's invitation, slowly subsided as I reconsidered the allure of the Kent coast at this time of year.

'Ha, well, it is very noble and selfless of you, Doctor, to undertake the journey on my behalf. I am certain that I could be relied upon to keep myself out of harm's way were you to decide to remain here in London, but at least it will save me the trouble of having to devise an excuse for your absence.'

Holmes's light-hearted banter proved to me that he had not been deceived by my spurious display of indignation in any way.

'Well, of course I shall come!' I laughed. 'However, it would be nice if you would consult me from time to time, upon such matters.'

'Excellent, so it is settled then.' With that Holmes turned sharply on his heels and led us briskly back towards Baker Street.

Holmes had reached our rooms several minutes before my arrival. The blinds had been pulled down to ward off the intense glare of the sun, and his sharp-featured profile was swathed in a grey shadow as the thick smoke from old shag pumped out into the room. He smiled towards me as I entered.

'When do you propose to depart for the coast?' I asked, whilst lighting up a pipe of my own.

'Well, we have an open invitation, however, there are certainly some arrangements that have to be made and, of course, there is still the small matter of the Egyptian Gargoyle to resolve,' Holmes replied thoughtfully. 'I suggest that we leave in three days' time, if that is agreeable to you.'

'That is more than agreeable, for it allows time for me to make arrangements for my patients with my accommodating neighbour, Dr Anstruther, who has filled that role on many occasions in the past. I had thought, however, that the matter of the Egyptian Gargoyle had already been brought to a satisfactory conclusion.'

'Oh, it has, Watson, I assure you. However, there are still one or two routine loose ends that need to be tied up. Lestrade has worked doggedly throughout this case, although his lack of vision almost led to the biggest fish slipping away from the lure. One final liaison with the good inspector will ensure that our work has not been in vain.

'Oh, Doctor, do put away your damnable notebook!' Holmes snapped when he saw my hand dipping into my inside breast pocket. 'I have already warned you that Mycroft will not brook any thoughts of this matter being made common knowledge until such time as it is safe to do so. There is too much at stake, you know.'

Naturally I obliged at once, for I was only too well aware of the influence that Holmes's brother wielded when it came to matters of state. Mycroft Holmes's position within the government was unique. His office acted as a form of brokerage, or exchange house, for all interdepartmental information whether it be trivial, or influential and far-reaching.

It was in this capacity that Mycroft was able to assimilate this information and, therefore, he had a profound influence on government policy. The two brothers and Inspector Lestrade were the only three people who were aware of the importance of the

Egyptian Gargoyle affair, so it was certainly not for me to make this knowledge public property.

At that precise moment Mrs Hudson arrived at our door and presented Holmes with a wire that she had been instructed to deliver urgently. Without a word to our poor landlady, Holmes snatched it from her grasp and tore it open ravenously. It only took a moment for him to digest its contents and he crumpled the sheet of paper into a tight ball before tossing it into the lifeless fireplace.

Holmes smiled contentedly to himself and rubbed his hands together gleefully, as if he had just been presented with his most sought after gift. Without another word, he dived into his room and for the next ten minutes I could hear the sound of him opening and closing drawers and cupboards, occasionally accompanied by a groan of impatience or frustration.

When he eventually emerged, even I, who had witnessed many such transformations take place, could not fail to be taken aback by the incarnation that now stood before me. Without a doubt, Sherlock Holmes now presented the perfect image of a very elderly street peddler.

Miraculously, he had reduced his height by a good six inches, his scarred face was lined and worn and his hair was now white, thin and bedraggled. Even his clothing was tarnished and threadbare and he carried a gnarled old cane together with a battered leather satchel.

Holmes laughed aloud when he observed the look of astonishment upon my face.

'In heaven's name, Watson, it is almost as if you do not recognize your old friend!'

'Were it not for your voice and the fact that no one else has passed this way, I could not swear to you being Sherlock Holmes,' I exclaimed. 'You have certainly surpassed yourself this time. However, it is disquieting to note that you still feel the need for such a subterfuge. This smacks of danger and not the routine tying up of loose ends that you predicted only a short time ago,' I added reproachfully.

'Do not concern yourself unduly, Watson, for I am just being overly cautious, I guarantee you. Rest assured I shall be in one piece when you see me next, at breakfast time tomorrow! Good day to you, Doctor.'

Holmes uttered these last words in the voice of a bronchial old man, merely to satisfy himself that he had achieved the correct tone. I assured him that he had and a second later he shuffled out of the room in full character. He did so with such effect, in fact, that Mrs Hudson let out a shrill shriek when she saw him leave the building.

I called down the stairs, to reassure her that it had only been her wayward tenant, whom she had seen hurriedly depart and nothing more sinister than that. I then set about planning our proposed trip.

Holmes had left Collier's letter conveniently on the table and, with the aid of my trusty Bradshaw, I soon ascertained that we needed to head towards Richborough, in southern Kent. I found this to be a most intriguing prospect as the surrounding area was, literally, steeped in sites of great historical interest.

Not the least of these was the ancient Roman fort that had guarded the port of Richborough for well over a millennium. The Roman Emperor Claudius had actually landed there when he first began his conquest of Britannia and, subsequently, the fort was rebuilt to ward off the marauding Saxons, over 300 years later.

Holmes had been correct when he had assured me that there was some decent fishing to be found in the surrounding area. Just down the road from Richborough was a small river that ran through the neighbouring village of Ash where I was guaranteed the best coarse fishing to be had in the entire county. The trip was becoming more appealing by the minute.

Then another prospect presented itself to me. I suddenly realized that an old friend of the family and a former colleague of my late father, had a large family home in the vicinity of Sandwich, which was just downriver from Richborough. I was certain that I would not be prevailing too much upon Holmes's indulgence, if I suggested a slight diversion, on our route to the Colliers, to pay a brief call upon Montague Abernetty and his family.

If Holmes was as good as his word and he was able to join me for breakfast, there was a late morning train from Charing Cross that would have us in Sandwich in time for lunch. Even if I were to spend a couple of hours in the company of my elderly friend, we would still be able to reach the Colliers before nightfall.

★   ★   ★

Completely satisfied that my arrangements were in place, I finally retired for the night convinced that Holmes would be agreeable to each one of them. Of course, that was before I came to realize the condition in which Holmes was to return from his mission. He was accurate in estimating the time of his return, but not in his prediction that his rendezvous with Lestrade was merely to 'tie up a few routine loose ends'.

He was able to creep up the stairs quietly enough, to avoid causing our landlady any further alarm. However, that did little to placate my own dismay when I saw him. His disguise was in complete disarray, his hat had completely disappeared and his wispy grey wig was stuffed into the pocket of his battered old coat. His trousers were splattered with mud and his face was cut in at least three separate places. However, it was the large gash upon his forehead that caused me the most concern.

Despite his efforts to shake me off, I soon had Holmes in his armchair and set to work on his wounds with some hot water, cotton wool and some iodine.

'In heaven's name, man, I shudder to think what state you would have returned in, had the matter not been so routine!' I protested.

Holmes waved this away with a flick of his fingers and began to fumble for a cigarette, with which I diligently supplied him.

'It is nothing of note!' he snapped impatiently.

'Naturally I understand that you will not be able to divulge the events of the past night to me without betraying your brother's confidences, but at least you can assure me that these are your only wounds, I hope,' I insisted.

'Scratches, Watson, these are merely scratches. That fool, Lestrade, almost let our bird escape, due to his inept arrangements, and, as you have witnessed, our quarry still had a further sting in his tail.'

Holmes spat out these last words bitterly, but I could see a smile slowly smoothing out the scowls of his supposed anger.

'Well, I am certainly glad to see that your injuries were not incurred in vain and that your night has ended in triumph,' I observed.

'You are quite correct, Doctor; the affair of the Egyptian Gargoyle is now no more! Once again the good inspector has garnered an ill deserved triumph on the back of my talent and humility.'

I could not help but laugh aloud at Holmes's clumsy attempt at modesty.

He joined me at once and soon proposed a Cognac while I described to him my plans for our trip to Kent. He listened diligently to each of them and nodded his agreement to them all.

'I will indulge your reunion with the Abernettys on condition that you promise to exclude me from all of your fishing expeditions. Moreover, as soon as Mycroft is convinced that the Egyptian Gargoyle affair has lost its sensitivity, I will provide you with a full and detailed account with which you can bore your readers.'

'I do not think that 'boring' is the adjective to use when describing my journals of your cases, but I am glad to see, from your humour, that you are in the right spirit in which to enjoy your sabbatical.' I smiled.

'In that case, when you have finally finished tinkering with my head, we can prepare for Charing Cross Station,' Holmes suggested, and, as soon I was convinced that the bleeding from his wound had congealed, we both set about our packing. It was pleasing to note that, in this instance, my army revolver was not to constitute a vital part of my luggage.

It was a mercy that Holmes's good-natured humour was to continue throughout that long and tedious journey. Our train, which left promptly from Charing Cross, seemed to stop at every conceivable station and I was convinced that we would both run out of tobacco long before we reached the station at Sandwich.

However, Holmes did not seem to be in the least bit put out by this endlessly long haul. Indeed, no doubt spurred on by my earlier passing reference to the Roman invasion of AD 43, he even began a discourse upon the subject of the evolution of the British people.

'You know, Watson, that it is almost inconceivable that a mongrel race, such as ours, is now responsible for an empire that encompasses over a third of the world's land mass. When you consider that at a time in history when great civilizations existed, both in the Far East and in places like Greece and Egypt, our race was running around in fur and daubing ourselves in blue paint; it is a transformation that is unique in history.

'As a race we have evolved and been influenced by peoples as diverse as the Romans and the Saxons. Each one planted their seeds and they are now bearing the fruit of the leaders of the world. There is certainly much to be said for being conquered as often as we have been. Oh yes, Watson, this trip of ours promises to be one of a most stimulating nature.'

I could not have agreed with him more. At that moment he sank into a silent reverie and he left me amazed once I realized that he had banished all thoughts of criminals and their nefarious deeds, as completely as I could have hoped for. By the time our train finally crawled into the station at Sandwich, the world's only amateur consulting detective had well and truly been left behind amidst the smoke and grime of our distant capital.

We despatched our trunks by way of a trap to the Colliers' address and then set off upon a delightful, leafy walk towards the home of the Abernettys. I could not recall the last time that I had seen my friend so relaxed and at peace with the world. His gait was slow and languid and he savoured the sight of each sage bush and swallow.

The drive, which we soon turned into, may not have been the longest that I have ever seen, but it was certainly the most fragrant. The strong sunlight could barely break through the leafy ceiling and all around us were row upon row of impressive firs and magnolia bushes. Once the drive opened up onto the gravel courtyard, we were met by an elegant line of Corinthian columns that guarded a wide set of grey marble steps.

To our surprise, the oak door to this Georgian mansion was hanging wide open. However, this was nothing when compared to our astonishment at the sight of an old friend standing at the head of the stairs — Inspector Stanley Hopkins!

Although he hailed from Brixton, in South London, Hopkins worked, for the most part, with the Kent police on cases of the utmost moment. He had been actively involved in as many as seven of Holmes's previous cases and, in Holmes's opinion, had always acquitted himself admirably. This was despite his having 'displayed a disappointing lack of imagination' while investigating the murder at the Abbey Grange.

Yet here the young detective stood, notebook in hand, outside the house of my old family friend, surrounded by an array of various vehicles that defied a reasonable explanation. Holmes and I exchanged a glance that told the other that our holiday was destined to be short-lived and we automatically increased the speed of our approach to the home of the Abernettys.

As soon as he had recognized us, Hopkins rushed down the stairs to greet us. He shook us both warmly by the hand, although the look of confusion and disbelief upon his face told us that we were the last people that he expected to see on that day.

'Well, upon my word, Mr Holmes, on this occasion you have certainly surpassed yourself with this timely arrival! Although how you managed to get here so quickly defies any rational justification. I was only summoned here myself barely an hour ago, and that was only a moment or two after the body was discovered.'

'So, it is a case of murder then?' I asked, sadly and apprehensively.

'Indeed it is, Doctor, and a strange

business it looks likely to be, for certain,' Hopkins confirmed.

Holmes placed a reassuring hand upon my shoulder.

'Oh, my dear fellow, be brave, for we must not assume the worst. The victim may prove to be a member of the staff,' Holmes offered as a half-hearted consolation. This, however, proved to be short-lived.

'The victim, I am afraid is old Montague Abernetty himself,' Hopkins announced. 'Although how you came to hear of it is beyond me,' he reiterated.

'As a rule I am loath to admit to the existence of such things,' Holmes replied. 'However, on this occasion, I can assure you, Inspector, that our impromptu arrival here is a result of nothing more uncanny than mere coincidence.' With that Holmes turned on his heels and strode off towards the house.

It fell on me, therefore, to explain to Hopkins the circumstances of our diversion to Sandwich and, of course, my connection to the Abernetty family. Hopkins was sympathetic when he heard of this, and, although I was not exactly close to the Abernettys, the news of Montague's untimely death rocked me back on my heels somewhat.

Hopkins and I followed Holmes to the house at a more sedate pace and, by the time that we had reached the garden at the rear of the house, Holmes was already on the ground by Abernetty's bath chair with his large lens held in front of him. He was oblivious to our arrival and we allowed him to continue with his work in uninterrupted silence.

As it transpired, this process was to be surprisingly short. Holmes emitted a loud grunt of disappointment and disgust and he then slammed his fist down into the dry turf at the old man's feet.

'Inspector!' he cried out. 'There are so many different traces around this area that the likelihood of my discovering anything worthwhile has long since been destroyed.' Holmes jumped up back to his feet and angrily brushed himself down.

'I can assure you, Mr Holmes, that nobody has been allowed to approach the body since my arrival, apart from the family physician, Dr Cardew. On my instruction he was most careful when he conducted his examination.' Hopkins was clearly taken aback by Holmes's harsh condemnation of his procedure and he did his best to defend himself.

This was clearly not lost on Holmes.

'Well, I suppose that the damage might have been done some time before you were summoned,' Holmes conceded in an apologetic tone.

Throughout this exchange I had just stood there staring at the body of a man whom I had known, on and off, since my early childhood. Despite the warmth of the afternoon sun, Abernetty's shoulders had been draped in a small tartan blanket and his chin was slumped down onto his chest. For a man of eighty-three years, he had a surprisingly full head of pure white hair and his mutton chops grew down to form a link to his bushy moustache.

To my dismay, however, the limited view that I had of his features revealed a face that had been contorted by pain and that the warm kindly smile, that I had always remembered of him, was now lost for ever.

'I presume Dr Cardew had been summoned prior to there being any thoughts of involving the police.' I broke off from my reverie with this obvious observation. 'After all, it is far from unusual for a man of his advanced years to pass away as a result of natural causes.'

'You are quite correct, Dr Watson. I was only called for once Dr Cardew's examination had revealed some unusual features that immediately raised his suspicions,' Hopkins confirmed.

'Are the remaining members of the household aware of these suspicions, or did

Dr Cardew take it upon himself to send for the authorities?' Holmes asked, while glancing around the garden.

'We were sent for only after Dr Cardew had consulted with Mrs Winifred Abernetty and the other members of her family. As you can see I have asked them all to remain indoors until such time as the body can be tactfully removed,' Hopkins confirmed and Holmes nodded his approval whilst moving towards the old man's tea tray.

'At what time did all this occur?' Holmes asked while motioning for me to write this down in my notebook.

'I was summoned at a quarter past the hour of three. This was exactly fifteen minutes after the doctor was called to the house,' Hopkins replied with his usual precision.

'So, therefore, death would have occurred before three o'clock?' Holmes asked next.

'Doctor Cardew would have to confirm the precise time of death, but that time would seem to fit the facts,' Hopkins confirmed.

'What were the unusual features that aroused Dr Cardew's suspicions in the first place?' I asked, while Holmes's fingers began to delicately manoeuvre the various items on the table that had been set up next to Abernetty's chair.

'It might be best if Cardew explains them to you himself. However, as far as I can gather, Dr Cardew carried out a thorough examination of Mr Abernetty only two days ago. Of course, the old man had lost the use of his legs some years ago and his mind was not as sharp as it once had been. However, in all other respects he found Abernetty to be in good general health.

'His death bears all the features of being the result of a severe heart attack, but in Dr Cardew's opinion the condition of Abernetty's heart was particularly good. That is why he recommended that the family send for the police and they lost little time in doing so, I must say,' Hopkins concluded.

Holmes had seemed to have been totally preoccupied with his own examination and I was not even sure that he had heard anything of my conversation with Inspector Hopkins. However, he turned towards us suddenly and glared at Hopkins with the utmost intensity.

'Were there no other reasons for Dr Cardew's uneasiness?' Holmes asked, with the air of one who already knew the answer to his question.

'As a matter of fact, there was something else, Mr Holmes. Although a doctor from within these small communities has a limited experience of such things, he was almost certain that there was a scent of almond around Abernetty's lips that he could not account for.'

Holmes gestured for me to examine Abernetty more closely.

'I know that it might prove to be unpleasant for you, old fellow, under these circumstances, but be assured that I would not ask it of you unless I felt that it were absolutely necessary,' Holmes said with quiet persuasion. 'After all, there is no one whose opinion I would value more,' he added, as if I would need any further bidding.

With some reticence I examined my father's old friend with as much discretion and delicacy as I was able. My search was a mercifully short one and my discovery proved to be as unpleasant as it was disturbing.

My suspicions were certainly aroused at the very mention of almond traces around the lips and I concentrated my search around the old man's face. I noticed at once that Abernetty's lips and tongue were unusually red and that his skin was deeply flushed. Of course, this last observation could have been attributed to the fact that Abernetty had spent many an hour outside in the glaring sun. However, in my view, the remainder of the evidence stood on its own and was conclusive.

Holmes voiced my concerns before I had even had the chance to expand upon my findings.

'Doctor, would it not be unusual to discover traces of almond around the lips of someone who has so obviously been consuming a plate of scones, butter and jam?' Holmes asked, while indicating the small tray that had occupied so much of his attention.

'Well, yes, of course,' I replied, after much consideration. 'However, there are other features here that are worthy of note. For example, assuming that the estimated time of Abernetty's death is an accurate one, rigor mortis has set in remarkably quickly. Death must have occurred instantaneously and, therefore, I deduce that it was not a result of natural causes.'

'So, in other words, you can confirm the findings of Dr Cardew, in that we are dealing with a case of murder?' Hopkins asked.

'Oh, most definitely,' I confirmed. 'Abernetty bears all the symptoms of having been poisoned with a small measure of cyanide, an unusual, yet lethal toxin that causes an instant and convulsive death. It is also very easy to disguise once it has been mixed into some food,' I added.

'So that would explain the contortions on Abernetty's face and his rapid change of skin colour. However, it is a strange substance to be found in an ordinary family home, is it not?' Hopkins asked.

I nodded my agreement.

'Whoever administered the poison certainly knew what he, or she, was about. Obviously the cyanide had been cleverly disguised amongst Abernetty's tea items. Yet it seems strange that the murderer would use a substance that would act so quickly and would, therefore, be likely to draw immediate attention to the cause of death,' I speculated.

I suddenly realized that Holmes had been unusually quiet throughout this entire conversation and I then saw that he was still preoccupied with Abernetty's tea tray. More specifically, he was intent upon his examination of the butter dish.

'Does it not strike you as peculiar that anybody would attach such urgency to the death of an apparently harmless old gentleman?' Holmes asked quietly, without turning away from his study.

'Are you implying that somebody within the household considered Abernetty to be some sort of threat to them?' Hopkins asked, in disbelief.

'At this stage I am not implying anything at all, Inspector. However you will agree that it is the only reasonable conclusion to be drawn from your analysis of the poison used. Ah, you see, Watson, I was attending to your every word, after all!' Holmes chided me.

'I did not doubt that for a minute, Holmes. Although I will say that you did seem to be somewhat preoccupied with your examination of Abernetty's tea tray. Has your study revealed anything of note?' I asked.

'Gentlemen, I will commend only this for your consideration.' Holmes presented this with the self-satisfied smile of a gourmet recommending a fine old wine to a dinner guest.

'A single pat of butter has already been consumed from this dish.' Holmes passed the dish to Hopkins and then to myself, in order that we might observe the small traces of butter at the edge of the dish from where it had been removed. Hopkins and I acknowledged our confirmation as Holmes carefully replaced it.

'Yet there are no traces of either scone or jam remaining,' Holmes continued. 'Therefore, we must conclude that there was sufficient butter, in just one pat, to accompany the other contents of the tray. Ah, I see that you think I am dwelling too much upon a matter of trivia.'

Evidently Holmes had detected an air of impatience and cynicism in my raised eyebrow and the exaggerated clearing of my throat.

'Well, it is hard to see the relevance and importance of this observation without further explanation,' I admitted grudgingly.

'The importance lies in the fact that this second pat of butter was not brought to the table at the same time as the first. We can confirm this because it is now a full two hours since the murder was committed and yet the sprig of parsley has hardly sunk into the butter at all! Therefore it was deliberately placed there to draw our attention away from the first,' Holmes concluded.

'Of course!' I exclaimed. 'That means that the poison was administered by somebody immersing it into the first pat of butter. The murderer could be sure that it would be used first because the other pat was not yet present on the dish.'

'Precisely, Watson. Oh, it took a few minutes to be sure, but I do believe that the penny has finally dropped. As I have told you, on many occasions, do not dismiss the finer details as nothing more important than mere trivia. This entire case could yet hinge upon a small sprig of decorative parsley and the timing of its delivery,' Holmes explained.

'Now I understand,' I responded sheepishly.

'Excellent, but I think we have kept the household waiting long enough. Gentlemen, I think it best if we interview each suspect individually, otherwise there is a danger that one person's reply might compromise the accuracy of another.

'However, Inspector, while they are all still together, I think it would be of benefit if you let it be known that the butter dish is to be kept securely in the cool of the larder, prior to my further examination of it in the morning,' Holmes suggested, as he handed the dish to the confused policeman.

'I would not pretend for an instant that I understand your reasons for asking this of me, Mr Holmes,' Hopkins replied. 'However, based on my previous experiences of your method, I would be a fool indeed if I did not act upon your every suggestion.'

With that, Inspector Hopkins led us towards the glass doors at the rear of the house, which opened into the drawing-room.

At this juncture an elderly gentleman with a severe stoop shuffled towards us from the door that we were approaching. This gentleman, I correctly concluded, was none other than Dr Cardew himself. The worn elbows of his hacking jacket seemed to indicate that his country practice was an exceptionally quiet one and, when he spoke, it was with a hushed, almost reverent tone. I moved forward and shook my colleague by the hand. He seemed quite abashed when I introduced Holmes to him and I lost little time in asking to confirm my findings.

'Oh, Dr Watson, you must understand that a small country practice, like mine, has very little experience of matters of this kind . . . ' His voice tailed away before Holmes interrupted him, somewhat impatiently.

'Yet you lost very little time in summoning the police, despite your lack of familiarity with criminal affairs. You were so certain that Mr Abernetty had not died of natural causes? After all, he was not a young man.'

Doctor Cardew was clearly taken aback by Holmes's sudden verbal assault and took a moment or two before making his hesitant response. Holmes could barely suppress a smile of malicious amusement when he observed the discomfort of the elderly practitioner.

'Mr Holmes, although I do not possess Dr Watson's expertise in such matters, I would be a poor doctor indeed if I had failed to recognize such obvious indications of foul play. Besides, I had cause to bring forward my regular house call, just two days ago, and I had found Mr Abernetty to be in the rudest of health.' Doctor Cardew smiled anxiously

116

towards my friend as he concluded his reply.

'Doctor Cardew, if you were not unduly concerned for the general good health of Mr Abernetty, what induced you to bring forward your regular visit?' Holmes asked next.

'Oh, but it was nothing at all. Mrs Abernetty had merely sent word to me that her supply of sleeping draught had run out prematurely. Therefore I had decided to kill two birds with one stone . . . eh, in a manner of speaking, of course.' Cardew cleared his throat nervously, once he had realized the indelicacy of his phrasing.

'Of course,' Holmes rejoined. 'I presume that Mrs Abernetty must be a poor sleeper, that she became so anxious at her lack of draught. Was this a normal occurrence?'

Doctor Cardew considered for a moment or two, before making his reply. 'She sleeps well enough at night, but in recent months she has come to rely on the draught in order that she can take the afternoon nap she so enjoys. However, this is the first time that I can recall her running out before the due date. I suppose that she must have misjudged one of her doses.'

'I suppose so,' Holmes said thoughtfully. 'Well, we must not keep you any longer, as I am certain that you have arrangements to make for the body.' Without another word

Holmes dismissed the doctor with a cursory wave of his hand and indicated that he wanted Hopkins to proceed to the drawing-room with the butter dish.

PART TWO

Conclusions

Holmes held me firmly by the elbow to ensure that Hopkins had plenty of time to make his announcement before we arrived in the room. We reached the drawing-room in time to see Hopkins taking the butter dish to the larder, holding it reverently in front of him as if it were the Holy Grail. Holmes smiled to himself when he observed the care that Hopkins was taking in carrying out his mission.

Hopkins returned a moment or two later, twirling the larder key around his finger, so that no one could be in any doubt that the butter dish was now securely locked away. I noticed that Holmes was keenly studying every face in the room, in the hope that he could perceive a significant reaction.

I leant towards him to suggest discreetly that he interview the widow, Winifred Abernetty, first of all. At her age, and due to her state of grief, I felt that she would benefit from returning to the cool of her bedroom as soon as was possible. Holmes agreed at once; however, it was also decided that her younger daughter, Clarissa, would stay behind to lend her mother her support.

In all honesty, she seemed to be a strange choice for this role, as she was taking the death of her father particularly badly and her sobbing was incessant and inconsolable. Indeed, Clarissa appeared to be receiving more support and comfort than her mother was and she could not be stilled throughout the entire interview.

The remaining members of the household were led from the room by an escort of two young constables who were under strict orders to ensure that nobody was to be allowed to leave the house until both Holmes and Hopkins had concluded their investigations.

This instruction was immediately met by an animated protest from the Abernettys' son-in-law, James Hastings-Thomas, who was destined to remain haughty and petulant throughout the entire process. The constables ignored his remonstrations with an admirably stoic silence and soon Hopkins, Holmes and I were alone in the quiet, shaded room with Winifred Abernetty and Clarissa.

It was hard for me to reconcile the frail, elderly woman opposite to me, with the robust, bombastic lady whom I had known for so many years. No doubt the untimely death of her husband had taken its toll on her constitution, but I also realized that my visit here had been long overdue and that her sharp decline was ultimately due to the ravages of time.

When Winifred spoke it was with a rasping voice, which barely rose above a whisper. Notwithstanding this, her daughter's continuous wailing rendered her words to be almost inaudible. I went over to her and placed a soft, respectful kiss upon the back of her outstretched hand and she stared back at me with a haunting look of despair.

'So, John, this is your celebrated friend, Mr Sherlock Holmes, I believe,' she stated simply.

'I am indeed Sherlock Holmes,' my friend replied, while bowing towards the tragic widow. 'You have my deepest sympathy and condolences, madam.'

'I thank you for them both,' Winifred replied. 'However, if you believe that I can enlighten you as to the cause and circumstances of my poor dear husband's demise, I am afraid that you are to be sorely disappointed.'

When she heard these words from her mother, Clarissa's sobbing moved up a decibel or two and it was several minutes before anyone in the room could either talk or hear.

'Why are you so certain that you cannot aid me in any way?' Holmes asked quietly.

'Simply put, Mr Holmes, I was resting in my room throughout the entire afternoon and was not even made aware of the tragedy until the inspector here made his timely and, might I say, sympathetic arrival. I wish I could shed some light upon the cause of my husband's death and I shudder at the thought of his murderer actually residing within my house!' The effort of putting this last sentence together caused Winifred to sink back into her chair and Clarissa's comforting arms were around her shoulders in an instant.

'I am afraid that my contribution will prove to be as slight as my mother's,' Clarissa said, while glancing towards Holmes over her shaking shoulders. 'You see, I was with her during the entire time that she was in her room and I supported her once she was finally summoned downstairs.'

'Did your mother not sleep at all while she was resting in her room?' Holmes asked, careful to exclude an accusing tone from his pointed question.

'She may well have drifted off from time to time.' When Clarissa replied to this with darting eyes, her grief miraculously subsided.

'So she would not have been aware had you decided to leave her room for a few moments?' Holmes persisted.

'Possibly not, but I can assure you, Mr Holmes, that I did not!' Clarissa replied determinedly.

'I am certainly most gratified to hear you say so. Was there anybody else in the house who was aware of your constant presence within your mother's room?' Holmes next asked.

'I would have had no way of knowing that for sure. However, it is a regular habit of mine to keep my mother company at that time of day. Now, if you have no further questions for either of us, I simply must take my mother back to her room. The strain of the events of this afternoon have weakened my mother's poor constitution considerably.' As she replied, Clarissa began to rise slowly from the arm of her mother's chair.

'With your permission, there is one last thing I need to ask of you.' Holmes smiled while holding up a restraining hand.

Reluctantly, and with some impatience, Clarissa took her seat once more.

'Mrs Abernetty, could you please tell me if you took a dose of your sleeping draught this afternoon?' Holmes asked quietly.

The elderly widow seemed to be somewhat taken aback by Holmes's strange question. Consequently, it was a moment or two before she made her reply.

'There is nothing unusual about that, Mr Holmes. I do find it difficult to fall into a deep sleep in the afternoon, and yet it is beneficial to my constitution. I have no need of it at night-time, but I do take it every day.'

'Are you certain that you take it every day?'

'Of course; I have just told you that I cannot sleep during the day without it.' Mrs Abernetty was becoming increasingly irritated by Holmes's persistent questioning. 'I allowed my supply to run out a couple of days ago, and I found myself incommoded as a result. However, I fail to see why this should be of interest to you.'

'Because Dr Cardew insists that this is the first time that it has ever occurred and I am always interested in the unusual. Where do you normally keep your supply?' Holmes's line of questioning was certainly raising a few eyebrows around the room, my own included. Mrs Abernetty replied, nonetheless.

'Why, in the top drawer of the cupboard next to my bed. I was certain that I had enough in there to last me until the doctor's next appointed call. However, I was disappointed to find the drawer empty the next time that I looked. I had obviously been mistaken.'

'Is there a possibility that another member

of the household might have taken some for their own use?' Holmes asked next.

'No, Mr Holmes, of course they would not! Why should they do so? Besides I spend so much time in my room that they would not have had the opportunity,' Mrs Abernetty replied indignantly.

'Except, at a time when you have already taken a sleeping draught. I understand that it induces a very deep sleep,' Holmes persisted.

'It does, indeed.'

'So, therefore, you would not have been aware if anyone had either entered, or left, your room.' As he finished this question Holmes raised an eyebrow in Clarissa's direction.

'No, I suppose not. Yet why should anyone decide to sneak into my room, merely to take a simple sleeping draught?' Mrs Abernetty shook her head in bewilderment.

'Why indeed,' Holmes confirmed.

Clarissa suddenly jumped up from her chair.

'Inspector, your Mr Sherlock Holmes is clearly exhausting my mother with his strange and incessant questions. Surely, under these circumstances, she might be allowed to return to her room for some rest?'

Hopkins glanced across to both Holmes and I for our acquiescence. Once we had nodded our agreement, Hopkins led them both to the door and Holmes excused the two women with a single gesture of his hand.

'Please stay by your mother's side constantly, for I might yet have further questions for you both,' Holmes requested.

'I can assure you, Mr Holmes, that there is nothing further that either of us can add to what we have already told you,' Winifred stated softly.

'Nevertheless . . . ' Holmes smiled.

The two grieving women shuffled slowly from the room.

'Well, Holmes, you could certainly have handled that situation more tactfully,' I complained, once I was certain that they were safely out of earshot.

'As you know, Watson, diplomacy never has been one of my stronger points. Besides, I found that there was something strangely exaggerated about the daughter's state of mourning.'

'Surely you do not suspect that poor girl of her father's murder?' I protested.

'At this point I would say that I suspect no one and everyone. I can only hope that we can learn some more from the subject of our next interview,' Holmes said, as he lit up a cigarette. He looked enquiringly towards the inspector who had remained silent throughout.

'I must confess, Mr Holmes, that I am also puzzled at the singular importance that you seem to attach to the missing sleeping draught. After all, it is a harmless enough substance, is it not?' Hopkins asked.

'Perhaps it is, and yet somebody within the household felt that it was important enough to secrete from within the bedroom of their matriarch. Mark this point well, gentlemen,' Holmes advised us.

Holmes appeared to be typically amused at the look of bewilderment on the faces of both Hopkins and myself. He then pulled on his cigarette and asked Hopkins to introduce the next subject for questioning.

'I have asked the elder daughter, Julie Hastings-Thomas to come and join us next,' Hopkins replied.

As I was turning the page of my notebook we heard a terrible commotion coming from the other side of the door. Despite the attempted restraint of one of Hopkins's constables, Julie's husband, James Hastings-Thomas somehow managed to force his way into the room.

'Now, what is all this nonsense about?' James demanded to know. 'You insist that my wife be subjected to your questioning, while I am excluded from the room. I simply will not allow it! As for this gentleman, who appears to be conducting this enquiry, well, I understand that he is not even on the official force. He is an amateur who has no right to be here at all!' James continued disdainfully, as he pointed an accusing finger directly towards Holmes.

'This gentleman happens to be Mr Sherlock Holmes who is here expressly at my invitation. Notwithstanding any knowledge that you might have of his enormous successes and his extraordinary abilities, I would strongly urge you to co-operate with him as fully as you can. There is nobody more qualified than he to get to the truth of the matter. I am certain that you are in favour of that, are you not?' There was a sceptical edge to Hopkins's last question that seemed to take the wind out of James's blustering.

'Er . . . well, yes, of course I am.' James replied hesitantly. 'However, my wife's nerves are somewhat frail at this particular time, and I will surely not interfere with your interview by sitting here at the back of the room.'

'That does seem to be a reasonable request, does it not, Mr Holmes?' Hopkins asked.

'Well, it will certainly save me some time and, besides, his presence might yet prove to be of some benefit,' Holmes replied, while staring at Hastings-Thomas with an unnerving intensity.

James acknowledged his thanks with a nod of his head towards Holmes.

'I apologize for my earlier boorish behaviour, Mr Holmes, but these are testing times for the entire family.'

'Now, madam, with as much clarity as you can manage, would you please recall for me your exact movements during the time leading up to the discovery of Mr Abernetty's body,' Holmes requested, with as much sympathy in his voice as a man of his nature could reasonably muster.

While the young lady gathered her thoughts, I could not but wonder at the remarkable difference between the behaviour and reaction of the two siblings in the face of their father's untimely death. As much as Clarissa was inconsolable and demonstrative in the extreme in the expression of her grief, so her sister, Julie, appeared to be cold and disaffected.

While her sister's appearance had been restrained, in fact almost dowdy, Julie was bedecked in the very latest fashion. Julie Hastings-Thomas was significantly taller than her sister and her elegant attire set off her striking head of rich auburn hair. She sat on the edge of a hard-backed chair with perfect posture, and appeared to possess a calm serenity that belied her situation.

'I will help you in any way that I can, Mr Holmes.' Her aloof tone seemed to signify her disdain at being questioned by a man whom her husband had just described as an amateur.

Holmes merely laughed at her haughty display.

'Then kindly be good enough to inform me of your precise movements over the course of the last two hours,' Holmes asked her intently and leant forward as he studied the eyes and features of the object of his questioning.

Julie Hastings-Thomas seemed to be somewhat taken aback by Holmes's abrupt change of humour and his sharp, official tone.

'I am not certain that I appreciate the manner in which you are studying me, Mr Holmes,' Julie said reproachfully.

'Oh, you must not mind me, madam; I am merely searching for the truth. Now please . . .' Holmes beckoned for her to respond to his original question.

'It will not be hard for me recount the last two hours or so because I was sitting in the library, totally engrossed in a book for most of that time. It was pleasantly cool in there and I am certain that I did not leave that room throughout the afternoon,' Julie replied calmly.

'I am certain that you fully understand the

reason behind our interview,' Holmes stated, with some irritation.

Julie nodded her confirmation emphatically.

'Well then,' Holmes continued, 'you must surely have realized that I need a more detailed account of your movements and actions right up to the time of your father's demise than the one with which you have just supplied me.'

'Surely you are not accusing my wife of having lied to you,' Hastings-Thomas said quietly, from the back of the room.

'No, sir, he is not!' Hopkins said this defiantly while glaring at Holmes for having made this premature implication.

'Well, perhaps there is somebody, within the house, who is able to corroborate your story?' Holmes asked, while smiling ironically. 'For example, maybe a servant brought some refreshment to you while you sat in the library, or performed another service?'

'We only have a small staff here, Mr Holmes, so we are quite used to fending for ourselves most of the time. I did leave the library for a few moments to make myself a pot of tea. However, I do not believe that I was observed, either on my way to or from the kitchen. Does this look bad for me?' Julie asked with surprising sarcasm.

Rather perversely, Holmes seemed to

prefer the cold, almost indifferent behaviour of Julie to the heartfelt declaration of grief of her sister. He smiled at her before asking his next question.

'Did your visit to the kitchen occur before or after your father's tea tray was delivered to him?'

'That question I can answer with some certainty, Mr Holmes. Mrs Barmby, who has been our cook for many years, is in the habit of preparing the tray for my father at two-thirty every day. As a rule she leaves it in the pantry ready for the page to deliver it in the garden at exactly three o'clock each afternoon. The tray was still there when I visited the kitchen,' she answered emphatically.

'Did you observe anybody who might have been able to interfere with the contents of the tray while you were there?' Although he was directing his questions at Julie, I noticed that Holmes's eyes had not strayed far from her husband from the minute that the couple had entered the room.

'I did not observe anybody, yet it is common knowledge that the tray is kept there and, therefore, anyone might have had access to it. Myself included, I suppose . . . ' Her voice tailed off when she made this last statement.

'I noticed that you refer to Mrs Barmby as

'our cook', yet I presume that you moved away from your family home following your nuptials,' Holmes said, while retaining his interest in Hastings-Thomas. Throughout this questioning I had observed him becoming increasingly uncomfortable at Holmes's constant attention. Hastings-Thomas did not voice these concerns, but he was constantly crossing and recrossing his legs, as his agitation steadily grew.

'My husband and I currently reside in a small, but comfortable house in St John's Wood. We undertook the journey to participate in my parents' anniversary celebrations, which have been lamentably cut so short.' Despite the poignancy of this last statement, Julie's icy demeanour did not waver, even for an instant.

'What would have been the nature of these celebrations, if they had taken place?' Holmes asked.

'Oh, nothing more exciting than a large dinner party, I am afraid to say. Many of the more prominent residents of Sandwich had been invited, if there are such things, Dr Cardew included. The house has been in a uproar for a week,' Julie replied disdainfully.

'I see, and so you decided to come down a week early to help with the preparations, I suppose?'

I could not, for the life of me, understand the motives behind some of Holmes's questioning. Nevertheless, I was certain that this would become clearer as the case progressed.

'Why, yes, of course we did!' Julie said indignantly.

'No doubt you also had much to discuss with your father. After all, since your marriage you must see very little of him and I am sure that you were always close. As close as your sister, would you say?'

'I am afraid, Mr Holmes, that such a thing is impossible to quantify. I suppose that Clarissa sees more of him, nowadays, although she has always rather doted on our mother. She was, undoubtedly, more supportive during that tawdry artist affair — '

I leant forward, at that moment, with my notebook in front of me.

'Excuse me, but we have not yet heard of the 'artist affair'. Perhaps you could provide us with some details,' I interrupted while indicating my pencil. She had spoken with the air of one who assumed that the affair in question was common knowledge.

'Is it absolutely necessary to plough that old furrow, once again?' Hastings-Thomas protested.

'If Mr Holmes is convinced of its relevance,

then I am afraid that it is essential that we do so,' Hopkins interjected on Holmes's behalf, no doubt hoping to avoid yet another tirade from the man.

'For argument's sake, we shall assume that it is relevant,' Holmes responded curtly.

At that moment Holmes was alerted to the fact that Hastings-Thomas was frantically scrabbling around for a light for his cigarette. Then, without a second's warning, and to the astonishment of everyone in the room, Holmes called out suddenly to Hasting-Thomas, 'Here you are, please try these!'

At once Holmes launched a silver box of vestas directly towards the man's face, with a surprising degree of force. Fortunately his target had the reflexes which allowed him to snatch the box with his right hand thereby preventing it from doing any damage. Not surprisingly, however, he appeared to be somewhat put out.

'Thank you, Mr Holmes.' Hasting-Thomas smiled ironically, and he made a point of lobbing the box gently back to Holmes, once he had made use of its contents.

Holmes seemed to ignore the entire incident and without a word of apology, he returned the box to his pocket. When I turned to glance at him, a second later, I observed, with some consternation, that he wore a smile of satisfaction. The thought processes of my enigmatic friend were impossible for me to fathom at times and this feeling was compounded when he resumed his questioning with an air of profound indifference.

Holmes turned his attention towards Julie, once more.

'Perhaps we should now hear about the affair of the artist,' he invited her.

'It was nothing really and hardly likely to have any bearing upon your investigation. I only mentioned it in passing so that you might fully appreciate how things stood between Clarissa and my father.'

Holmes crossed his legs and lit a cigarette while he smiled encouragingly at the young lady.

'I am certain that your statement will prove to be of the utmost interest and importance,' he said, although I was by no means convinced of his sincerity.

'The artist in question was a young bohemian named Stephen Possney. Despite his lack of success and, dare I say, any real talent, my sister was absolutely besotted with the man. He was a disciple of the Pre-Raphaelite school and was constantly searching for the means to establish his own studio.

'There was little doubt in my mind that Possney was merely romancing my sister out of her dowry and that her love was not reciprocated. Personally speaking, I never did understand what it was that she saw in the fellow. However, she would not be dissuaded and within a short time she had accepted his proposal of marriage.

'Here, however, my father stood firm. He would not see his daughter involved with such a scoundrel. He refused to release to her a single penny of her dowry until he was certain that it would not be squandered on a 'foolish artist's dream'. It was no surprise to any of us when Possney suddenly disappeared upon hearing of our father's decision. However, Clarissa was heartbroken and vowed that she would never forgive Father for destroying her only chance of happiness.'

Julie certainly seemed to be very satisfied with herself upon completion of her brief narrative, and I could not help but wonder at her motive for creating such mischief for her sister. She smiled maliciously at Holmes and seemed disappointed to note that he had now turned his attention towards her husband, without making a single comment regarding her version of the Possney affair.

'Now, Mr Hastings-Thomas, perhaps you would kindly explain to us your exact movements during the hours leading up to the discovery of your father-in-law's body,' Holmes requested.

'If you are expecting me to furnish you with the type of irrelevant gossip that you encouraged from my wife, then you are to be disappointed, I am afraid. My afternoon was very simply spent. I had been informed that the best coarse fishing in the county was to be found on the nearby River Ash. I decided to make an early start of it and consequently I returned at a little after two o'clock.'

'I, too, have been informed that there is good sport to be had there,' I confirmed with an emphatic nod of the head, at which point Holmes raised his eyes despairingly to the ceiling.

'Did anybody see you depart this morning, or return this afternoon?' Holmes asked, much to Hastings-Thomas's annoyance.

'Obviously, I did not travel down from London with my line and tackle, so Granville, the young page, furnished me with them both. He will also be able to confirm the time of my departure.'

'It would be more pertinent if he could confirm the time of your return, would it not?' Holmes continued.

'Well there, unfortunately, I cannot help you, Mr Holmes. The strange thing is that when I did finally return, Granville was nowhere to be found. Nor has he been seen by anyone since the time of my departure.'

'I see, and nobody thought this to be an important enough fact to bring to my attention earlier?' Holmes glared at Hopkins who simply shrugged his shoulders apologetically.

'Has a concerted search been instigated for the young lad?' Holmes asked of both the inspector and Hastings-Thomas.

'I searched for him myself as soon as I returned from my fishing trip, as I wished him to relieve me of my tackle and rod. However, the mystery of his disappearance continued well into the afternoon and, in Granville's absence, I had to deliver old Abernetty's tea tray to him myself. In any event, I returned before three o'clock, as that is the time when Abernetty usually took his tea,' Hastings-Thomas concluded.

Holmes sat silently for a moment, while he contemplated his next question. He placed his right forefinger on his lips and stared vacantly towards an empty corner of the room.

'Can I assume that my wife and I are now excused, Inspector?' Hastings-Thomas asked, while rising from his chair.

'Mr Holmes, have you completed this

interview?' Hopkins asked anxiously, obviously as confused as the rest as to the reason behind Holmes's protracted silence.

'Ah yes, of course ... the interview. I apologize for my distraction. Were there no other servants available for the task of delivering the tray to Mr Abernetty? After all, I am sure that the page was not the only person capable of carrying out such a task,' Holmes asked, with an edge of sarcasm to his question. 'Or perhaps there was another reason for your being so obliging?'

'I take exception to the tone of your questioning, Mr Holmes,' Hastings-Thomas protested. 'However, as it so happens, I was the only person available at that time. Mrs Barmby had gone down to the village to ensure that she had sufficient vegetables for tonight's celebration. I also knew that Archer and the maid were busy putting the finishing touches to the dining-room. I am certain that they are all willing and able to corroborate my story,' he added hastily.

'I am sure that they are. In that case I see no good reason for continuing our delightful conversation.' Holmes turned to Hopkins and, with a dismissive wave of his hand, indicated that he should escort the couple from the room.

'Well, I must say, you are the rudest

fellow — ' Hastings-Thomas was unable to complete his sentence because Hopkins hustled them from the room with the utmost urgency. Once Hopkins had returned to his seat, both he and I were dismayed to note that Holmes was sitting there rubbing his hands together gleefully and triumphantly.

'Well, that conversation proved to be most instructive, would you not say?' Holmes asked, with an air of expectation.

'You have evidently learnt a great deal more from it than either the good doctor or myself,' Hopkins replied.

'Yet we have all heard and digested the same information,' Holmes replied.

'Indeed, so perhaps you would care to enlighten us before we interview the staff,' Hopkins suggested.

'Well, yes, of course, but surely you have both formulated your own opinions, upon the matter.'

Hopkins referred to his notes and came to the same conclusion that I had done.

'It seems to me that every member of the household had the opportunity to administer the poison at some point during the afternoon. Clarissa could have left her mother's side while the old lady took her afternoon nap; Julie has already admitted that she went to the kitchen to fetch some refreshment, and her husband actually delivered the tray to Abernetty himself.

'So it really comes down to the motive. From what we have heard, Clarissa had both motive and opportunity. To a young woman, there is no greater validation than the loss of her one true love. Besides which, we all agreed that her display of grief appeared to be somewhat exaggerated. No, I do not think that we need to look any further than Clarissa Abernetty,' Hopkins boldly proclaimed.

Not surprisingly, considering his long held views upon the subject, Holmes appeared to be suitably amused when Hopkins made mention of Clarissa's doomed romance being her motive for murder. He lit a cigarette and turned to me for my assessment of the statements that we had heard so far.

'I have to agree with the good inspector, here. As far as I can judge, nobody, other than Clarissa, appears to have had a good reason for wishing the old man dead. Besides, if either Hastings-Thomas or his wife had carried out the deed, I cannot believe that they would have implicated themselves in the way that they have done. As for the staff, well, they all seem to have adequate explanations for their movements at the time of the murder,' I concluded.

'Apart, that is, from the young page!'

Holmes exclaimed. 'Do neither of you regard the timing of his disappearance as being in the least bit significant?' Holmes asked, looking back and forth from Hopkins to me.

'Young lads are not always the most reliable of servants,' I ventured. 'Perhaps we might learn more about his character and general behaviour once we begin to interview the other members of the staff.'

'Ah, yes, of course.' Again Holmes appeared to be strangely distracted and I received the distinct impression that he viewed their forthcoming statements with a profound indifference. 'However, before we usher the staff in here, I would commend one further observation to your attention,' Holmes continued. 'You are both too dismissive of the possibility of the involvement of the Hastings-Thomases. Do you not regard a scarcity of funds as an adequate motive for murder?'

'Well, yes, of course I do. However, there are no obvious indications that this is the case,' I replied.

'On the contrary, I could identify at least five or six.' Holmes smiled broadly as he made this dramatic assertion. He slowly leant back into his chair and he clearly enjoyed watching our reaction to his bold statement.

'For example, if you had studied the patches upon Hastings-Thomas's jacket sleeve, you would have seen that the stitching around them was not the original. Therefore, they had been added at a later date, more out of necessity than to his tailor's statement of style.'

'You mean to say that he had worn out his elbows?' I asked incredulously.

Holmes nodded his head emphatically.

'Do not allow yourself to be taken in by his brusque and cavalier persona,' Holmes warned. 'That couple have, assuredly, fallen on hard times. Julie's deportment is that of a member of high society and yet her costume is at least three seasons out of date. The ends of her narrow heels have been replaced on three separate occasions that I can see, and her jewellery has not been cleaned in years. Do you think that I need to continue?'

'You have certainly made your point well, Mr Holmes,' Hopkins confirmed. 'However, this analysis of yours hardly makes the situation any clearer . . . to me.'

'Perhaps not, but at least it has opened your eyes to other possibilities. That couple do not appear to be the type of people who would readily set their hands to the preparations for a party. So, we have to ask ourselves whether they had other reasons for their early arrival. How much in need were they of a helping financial hand from Julie's late father?' Holmes pondered.

'As you say, Mr Holmes, there are other possibilities,' Hopkins agreed. 'Perhaps the household staff can shed some more light on the mystery. I have asked Mrs Barmby, the cook, to step in first. At her age the strain of the day's events have taken their toll on her nerves and she is in urgent need of some rest.'

'That is a most admirable suggestion, Inspector,' Holmes acceded.

Hopkins was on the point of despatching his constable for the fragile-sounding cook when a rather fetching young parlour maid burst suddenly into the room, seemingly in a state of great agitation. She stood, rooted to the spot, by the French windows that she had just come through and stared at each one of us in turn, while she tried to catch her breath.

'Well, what is it, girl?' Hopkins gently enquired.

'Beggin' your pardon, gentlemen, but it is the page boy, Granville. We have found him . . . asleep in the potting shed!' When she spoke it was with a delightfully light Scottish lilt that belied the urgency of the situation.

'Asleep?' I exclaimed. 'Had he been drinking?'

'Oh, no, sir, he comes from a righteous family and his father was a chaplain. It was only the sudden death of his father that forced Granville into service in the first place,' the girl protested.

Not surprisingly, it was Holmes who was the first of us to react and, in an instant, he sprang out of his chair and he was leap-frogging over the back of a low *chaise-longue* towards the garden before Hopkins and I had even stirred.

'Hurry, Doctor, and bring your bag!' Holmes called out over his shoulder.

We followed him an instant later and by the time that we had reached the potting shed, the young page was already back on his feet. Granville was a tall, gangling youth and he stood there, as if in a daze, repeatedly and vigorously rubbing his red eyes. I could see that the page's legs could barely hold him up and I helped him back down to the ground, so that he could lean against the shed wall.

'I do not know what happened to me, sir, I really do not.' Granville's voice was low and decidedly unsteady and he was clearly embarrassed by what had occurred to him.

We allowed him a few moments more so that he might further recover his senses, before Holmes gently asked him to explain the events that had led to his incapacity.

'Mr Archer sent me down here to fetch up a small selection of flowers with which to decorate the dining-table for tonight's celebrations. It is the Abernettys' wedding anniversary, you know.' Granville looked up to me proudly, as if he had just passed on the very latest news. I smiled and nodded my confirmation.

'Anyhow, I was loading up a large steel tray with some pots when the urgent need to sit down and a wave of light-headiness came upon me. I carefully placed the tray upon the ground and sank down right next to it. The very next thing I knew was that Claire was shaking me by the shoulders trying to wake me up. I have never felt so tired, you know. Here, who took the tea tray out to Mr Abernetty? I'll be lucky if I still have a job after this.' Granville shook his head from side to side disconsolately as he pondered his predicament.

'I should not worry about that, if I were you. Mr Hastings-Thomas delivered the tray, so there is no real harm done,' I consoled him.

'No real harm done?' Granville exclaimed. 'The very idea of a gentleman like Mr Hastings-Thomas delivering a tray — what a thought! Mind you, he must have come back from his fishing pretty sharpish.' Granville began to shake his head once more. 'I must apologize to Mr Abernetty at once. I really do not know what came over me, sir, I really do not.'

He attempted to drag himself back off the ground, but a gentle and restraining hand upon his shoulder was enough for me to be able to prevent this from happening. Holmes gestured for me to examine Granville's eyes and it was only then that the page realized that we were strangers to him.

'Who are you gentlemen anyway?' he asked, and his voice became stronger as his consciousness slowly returned to him.

'My name is Sherlock Holmes and I am afraid that my friend and colleague, Dr Watson, here, has some rather unfortunate news for you.' I was somewhat put out at the sight of Holmes turning on his heels and walking back towards the drawing-room doors, leaving me with the unenviable task of informing the young man of the death of his employer.

It took a moment or two for this news to sink in, but, once it had done, I could see that the young lad was clearly upset by this tragedy.

'Poor Mr Abernetty,' he repeated quietly to himself and, after a while, I decided that he would be better off in his room to which Claire gently guided him.

I saw Holmes leaning against the back wall of the house smoking a pipe and lost in deep thought. Hopkins and I joined him there and

Holmes immediately sought my opinion upon the incident of the page.

It did not take me long to reach and then express my conclusions.

'I am in little doubt that Granville's sleep was not a natural one. One look into his eyes and the manner in which he described his gradual collapse convinces me that some form of sleeping draught found its way into his food, or drink. The manner in which this was achieved I cannot say, but he is certainly not our murderer,' I declared.

'Well, of course not, he was asleep at the time when the deed was done,' Holmes snapped. 'However, the administrator of the draught undoubtedly is.'

'We cannot be certain of that, Mr Holmes,' Hopkins quietly objected.

Holmes considered the inspector thoughtfully for a moment before making his reply.

'Consider, if you will, how unlikely a coincidence it would be if that were not the case. Mrs Abernetty's sleeping draught disappears from her room just two days before her husband is murdered and it is then used against the very person who was supposed to have delivered the fatal tray to the victim. As I have told Watson on many an occasion, once you have eliminated the impossible, whatever remains, no matter how improbable, has to be the truth. The likelihood of the two incidents being unconnected is an impossible one. The question we should ask is, who stole the sleeping draught in the first place?' Holmes spread out his arms invitingly and awaited our response.

'Well, Hastings-Thomas eventually delivered the tray, so perhaps this had been arranged by design,' Hopkins offered. 'However, the butter may have already been tampered with before he had even returned from his fishing expedition and Granville provided him with the tackle before his departure . . . ' His voice tailed away as he reconsidered his position.

'Would not his presence in the old lady's bedroom have aroused unnecessary suspicions amongst other members of the household?' I ventured.

'Excellent, Watson! However your deduction hardly narrows down our field.'

'Surely it serves to reaffirm my view that Clarissa must be our principal suspect. After all, it would have been perfectly natural for her to be in her mother's bedroom and she would have known exactly where to look for the sleeping draught,' I persisted.

'Watson, whilst there is certainly a confused logic behind your reasoning, I must point out to you that the draught would have been completely useless to her if Clarissa had no intention of delivering the tea tray herself.

'Besides, we have yet to establish whether she would have had the opportunity to administer the draught to the page. By her own admission, she spent the entire afternoon in the company of her mother. No, I am afraid that we need to look in an entirely different direction if we intend to catch our killer,' Holmes concluded.

'Gentlemen, may I remind you both that Mrs Barmby has been patiently awaiting our pleasure in the drawing-room, while we have been theorizing out here?' Hopkins pointed out politely.

I turned towards the house and then realized that Holmes was walking in the opposite direction.

'Would you both mind terribly if I leave the remaining interviews in your very capable hands? I believe that a turn around these charming gardens would be infinitely more beneficial to me. I am certain that if anything of note comes to light, Dr Watson will have detailed notes to pass on to me.' With that, Holmes doffed his hat, lit a cigarette and made off towards the nearest hedgerow.

Hopkins and I shrugged at each other and returned to the drawing-room. As it transpired, Mrs Barmby had run out of patience long before our return, and had returned to her duties in the kitchen, no doubt devising ways of using up her considerable excess of vegetables. Until Mrs Barmby could be persuaded to join us, we contented ourselves by questioning both Archer, the butler, and the young maid who had brought us the news of Granville's discovery.

Unfortunately they could only confirm the information that we had already heard from the others. They had been working together in the dining-room throughout the time leading up to the discovery of poor Abernetty's dead body. It was only once everything for the proposed celebration was in readiness that Archer had sent Granville down for the flowers. Of course, the length of time that Granville had been gone eventually aroused their suspicions and it was only when they instigated a search for the page that they had been informed of the murder of their employer.

Consequently, they could not confirm or deny the alleged movements of any members of the family. They did not know of Hastings-Thomas's fishing trip, although Archer did think it strange when he found a rod and some tackle strewn in the entrance hall.

Granville normally took his own tea, just

prior to delivering the tray to Abernetty, so we concluded that the draught must have been disguised in Granville's drink. The guilty party, of course, still remained a mystery. Archer and the maid were clearly upset by the news of their employer's untimely demise, which only served to confirm Abernetty's popularity amongst his servants. Other than that, we were to learn nothing of note.

Finally Mrs Barmby was persuaded to return to the drawing-room, where both Hopkins and I offered her our sincerest of apologies, which she accepted gracelessly. She had been clearly moved by the death of Abernetty and although they were now dry, her eyes were both red and raw. She was a short, rotund lady, and her round kindly face and her silver hair gave her a most matronly appearance. Her blue apron was splattered with flour, which augured well for the evening meal that lay ahead.

'I have not got the time to sit here nattering with the likes of you,' she complained. 'My poor master's celebrations may have been cancelled, but there are still enough of you to prepare dinner for. It will not cook itself, you know.'

'No, of course it will not.' Hopkins smiled his agreement. 'There are only one or two things that we need you to help us with.'

Mrs Barmby was clearly affected by Hopkins's cleverly chosen words and her attitude towards us changed once she believed that her contribution was potentially important.

'Naturally, I will help you gentlemen in any way that I can,' she announced proudly.

'We understand that you were in the village, shopping for extra vegetables, in the hour before Mr Abernetty's death was discovered.' Hopkins nodded his appreciation before putting this to her.

'You can't have too many vegetables, I always say,' the cook confirmed.

'Can you tell us if you had prepared Mr Abernetty's tea tray before you departed for the village?' Hopkins asked.

'I most certainly did, sir. Mr Abernetty is . . . I mean, *was*, most particular about taking his tea at the same time every day. I made sure that everything was ready to take out to him at three o'clock precisely and left instructions with young Granville.' Mrs Barmby touched the corner of each eye with her handkerchief once she realized that she had referred to her former employer in the present tense.

'Take your time, Mrs Barmby. We understand that this is most distressing for you.' I quietly attempted to console her.

'Thank you.' She smiled. 'Oh, he was such a dear man.'

'Were you aware of the whereabouts of other members of the household before you departed for the village?' Hopkins asked of her, once she had calmed herself.

'I left Mr Archer and Claire in the dining-room making their final preparations, and Granville was running errands for them when I reminded him about the tea tray. As for the family . . . well, I am certain that Miss Clarissa was sitting with her mother; she would not dream of leaving her whilst she was asleep. They are very close, you see.'

'So I understand,' Hopkins confirmed. 'Do you remember the whereabouts of both Mr and Mrs Hastings-Thomas?'

'I know that the gentleman had gone off quite early in the morning and that he had not returned by the time that I had left for the village. Miss Julie, however, was keeping out of the sun by spending her afternoon in the library.' Mrs Barmby appeared to be quite proud of the fact that I was busy writing down everything that she had said.

'Did you notice if she had any refreshments with her while she was reading?' I asked, as I tried to confirm Julie's story.

'Not that I could see, although I could tell

that somebody had helped themselves to some tea while I had been out. I would never have left my kitchen in such a state,' Mrs Barmby insisted.

'So, either of them could have had easy access to Mr Abernetty's tray during your absence?' Hopkins concluded.

'Well, it was not exactly kept under lock and key! Who would have thought that such a shocking thing was going to happen?' The cook appeared to be becoming quite agitated once again, at the notion of her being responsible, in some convoluted way, for the tragedy.

'Who indeed?' Hopkins paused for a moment, before asking his next question.

'What about Granville's tea? Did you prepare it for him before you went out?'

'Of course I did. Who else would do it for him? Here, you're not implying that I put anything funny in it, are you?' Mrs Barmby protested.

'No, of course I'm not.' Hopkins smiled charmingly. 'However, I would like to know if you noticed anybody else near the kitchen just before you left.'

'No, sir, everybody was where I said. One thing I should tell you though . . . ' The cook's voice suddenly dropped to a confidential whisper. 'Yesterday afternoon I did see

Mr Hastings-Thomas become quite agitated with Mr Abernetty over some letter or other. I could not tell you what it was about, but Mr Hastings-Thomas tried to grab it from the old man. Mr Abernetty was having none of it, though, and thrust the envelope back into his jacket pocket.'

'Did they raise their voices?' Hopkins asked.

'I could not be sure because they were in the garden at the time, and I only saw then through the pantry window. They did seem to be upset though, that I can tell you.'

'Thank you, Mrs Barmby, that could prove to be most useful to us. Is there anything else that you can add?' Hopkins asked.

She shook her head thoughtfully, for a moment or two.

'No doubt you gentlemen would like something to eat for your supper.'

Hopkins and I both nodded emphatically.

'In that case you had better let me get back to my kitchen.' The cook rose to leave and we thanked her enthusiastically for her assistance.

Before we began to search for Holmes in the garden, I sat silently going through my notes while Hopkins smoked thoughtfully from his pipe.

'Well, that was not a complete waste of

time and everybody's stories seem to be born out by her evidence,' the inspector observed.

'We are also now in possession of another motive that certainly seems to implicate Hastings-Thomas,' I pronounced.

'If you are referring to the tussle for the letter, I am afraid that you are certainly wide of the mark.' At that moment a familiar voice rang out from behind the drawing-room door and Sherlock Holmes peered in from behind the curtains.

'Holmes!' I exclaimed. 'Would you mind telling me how long you have been eaves-dropping? Are my notes now to be deemed as redundant?'

'No, not at all, old fellow,' Holmes responded, as he joined us in the room. 'I was only there long enough to hear of the incident of the letter. The remainder of your observations will, no doubt, prove to be as invaluable to me as they always are.'

'Well, I am certainly glad to hear it. However, I would like to know why you do not regard the incident of the letter as a worthwhile motive that would implicate Hastings-Thomas,' I demanded.

'Oh, Watson, I don't understand why it is that sometimes it is the most simple of solutions that you find the most elusive. I do not dismiss the letter as a matter of trivia, but for the nature of the true motive we shall have to search in far deeper channels. You are both forgetting one thing, namely the fact that the sleeping draught had disappeared from Mrs Abernetty's drawer a full twenty-four hours before the incident in the garden.' Holmes glared at each of us in turn, his frustration evidently increasing with each passing second.

'You forget that the reason for Dr Cardew's unscheduled visit was not to examine the old man's heart, but to replenish Mrs Abernetty's supply of sleeping draught which had run out a day earlier than he had expected,' Holmes reminded us.

'Of course!' I exclaimed. 'Therefore, if Hastings-Thomas did have a reason to steal the draught, it existed before he confronted Abernetty with the letter.'

Holmes threw back his head in exasperation.

'So there is some capacity for reasoning somewhere inside there,' Holmes laughed, while pointing towards my head.

I was on the point of restating my case for Clarissa having the only obvious motive, when the welcome sound of the dinner gong brought our review of the case to a temporary conclusion.

Understandably, the dinner for which we had all gathered together was a silent and joyless affair. The preparations for the planned celebrations were still very much in evidence within the dining-room. The oak-panelled room positively sparkled in every corner and the best silver glimmered brightly upon the large rosewood table.

The meal itself consisted of a country vegetable soup, followed by a huge rack of lamb and a delicious greengage tart. The wines were well chosen from the cellar and the service, provided by Archer and the maid, was impeccable. Yet my friend appeared to be oblivious to it all, as he just sat there refusing each course, in turn, whilst studying the faces of each one of the dinner guests.

Our hostess sat at the head of the table, frail-looking and ashen, while her daughters sat on either side of her, each of them gently cajoling her into taking some food. She accepted it reluctantly, and her eyes did not leave the small portrait of her husband that hung on the wall opposite.

As we had sat down I had asked Claire as to the welfare of Granville, the page. Apparently he was now fully recovered and would shortly be assisting Mrs Barmby in the kitchen. Otherwise the meal was taken in silence. Finally this was broken by Hastings-Thomas as the meat plates were being cleared away.

'Is the food not to your taste, Mr Holmes?' he asked disdainfully, upon observing Holmes's abstinence.

Holmes did not reply to this subtle rebuke, but with Mrs Abernetty's permission, merely lit up a cigarette and continued his study of the sombre family. I took it upon myself to answer on Holmes's behalf.

'Very often, during the course of an investigation, Mr Holmes refrains from sustenance until the case is concluded, as he regards it as a distraction and a waste of the energy that his subtle faculties require.'

Holmes laughed softly, under his breath.

'Well said, Watson ... subtle faculties indeed!'

'Can you inform us of any progress that you and the good inspector have made so far? After all, we cannot remain confined to the house indefinitely. Who is to know how long it will take your 'subtle faculties' to unravel our little mystery.'

By now I was finding the haughty mannerisms of Hastings-Thomas tiresome in the extreme. However, Hopkins saved me the trouble of having to rebuke him.

'You would do well not to trivialize the gravity of the situation, sir. After all, each one of you is under suspicion for the most serious of crimes. Therefore, not one of you will be allowed to leave these four walls until Mr Holmes and I decide that it is appropriate for you to do so. Do I make myself clear?'

'Oh, absolutely clear, although I cannot understand why the staff has been excluded from this web of suspicion. After all, they had as much opportunity to tamper with Abernetty's food as the rest of us, perhaps even more,' Hastings-Thomas persisted.

'Mr Hastings-Thomas, unless you have anything to fear, I am certain that another twenty-four hours will not matter to you either one way or the other,' Holmes announced gravely while facing his inquisitor for the first time since the meal had begun.

'You are so certain that the matter will be resolved within that time?' Hopkins asked Holmes incredulously.

'I am.'

'In that case, would you mind informing us of the direction in which your investigation is leading?' Hastings-Thomas asked.

'That I am not at liberty to divulge. However, I can inform you, with some certainty, that the affair will be resolved by the morning,' Holmes told us, while extinguishing a cigarette in his tart!

At this point Mrs Abernetty began to raise herself gingerly from her chair.

'You are both an arrogant and impudent

young fellow, Mr Holmes!' she pronounced and, without another word and with Clarissa in close attendance, she made her way from the table.

'I apologize if I have offended you, madam,' Holmes called out before the matriarch had reached the door. 'Unfortunately the path towards the truth can sometimes be a most uneven and painful one.'

Mrs Abernetty glared angrily towards him, but, without another word, she took hold of Clarissa's arm and shuffled from the room. A short while later Hastings-Thomas and his wife joined them, leaving Holmes, Hopkins and myself to our port and cigars.

'You really are the most inscrutable fellow, Mr Holmes,' Hopkins ventured through a plume of cigar smoke. 'After all, it would do the investigation no harm were you to divulge to Watson and myself some of your ideas upon the matter.'

'I have revealed little to you so far for the simple reason that, at this moment, there is precious little to reveal. Everybody seems to be telling the truth, so far as I can judge; therefore, we have to decide what it is that has been withheld and by whom,' Holmes replied.

'Holmes, it seems strange, does it not, that

anybody would steal the sleeping draught if they had no intention of using it for another two days? Surely that action would arouse unnecessary and premature suspicion,' I speculated.

'Perhaps they did not think that they would get another opportunity to remove it. Remember it is only Clarissa who has constant access to her mother's room. We have to ask ourselves whose presence in the old lady's room would have looked the most out of place.

'Obviously that brings us back to Hastings-Thomas. In the case of the two daughters it would look out of place if they did not visit their mother regularly. The staff, of course, could adopt any pretext for carrying out a chore in there at any time. Although there is another . . . ' Holmes's voice mysteriously tailed away.

'Everything seems to support your case against Hastings-Thomas and yet Clarissa still appears to possess the strongest motive. If only we knew the contents of that letter,' I complained.

'There was no sign of it amongst the old man's possessions,' Hopkins confirmed.

'Well, then, it must be in the possession of the murderer!' I proclaimed, although, of course, I realized as soon as I had made this statement, that if the letter had contained any incriminating information it would surely have been destroyed by this time.

I glanced towards my friend and soon saw from his expression that he, too, had noticed the weakness behind my reasoning. He hurled the remains of his cigar into the fireplace and immediately filled up his cherry-wood. He drew deeply from his pipe and watched the heavy smoke drift slowly towards the open window, as if this was the first time that he had ever lit a pipe.

'This case is not yet clear to me,' he announced solemnly. 'My senses have been blinded by the most obvious of conclusions.'

'Whatever do you mean?' I queried.

'Inspector Hopkins, do you recall the case of Morgan the Poisoner?' Holmes asked surprisingly.

'Yes I do, although, of course, I was not actively involved in the investigation. It appeared in all the daily papers and created a tremendous stir as the fellow could not be convicted, despite there being a strong case against him. If I remember correctly, a piece of vital evidence went missing during the course of the trial.' Despite his assured reply, Hopkins clearly failed to fathom the reason behind Holmes's question.

'Your memory evidently serves you well,

Inspector. I, too, was not involved with that case as it occurred during my sojourn in Tibet; however, I did read up on it once I returned. The piece of missing evidence was, interestingly enough, the remains of the arsenic with which Morgan had allegedly murdered his wife.'

At that moment Holmes was interrupted by Archer, the butler, who came to enquire as to whether we would like a pot of coffee to conclude the meal.

As Archer was turning to leave to get our drinks, Holmes suddenly called him back.

'Archer, do you recall Dr Cardew's visit of two days ago?'

'Oh, indeed I do, sir. I let him in myself,' the butler confirmed.

'So you will, no doubt, be able to tell me how long he remained here?' The reason behind Holmes's unusual questioning was totally beyond me.

'I believe that he came to deliver an urgent package that Mrs Abernetty had been waiting for. I offered him some tea, but he told me that he was in too much of a hurry to stay. I would say that he was here no longer than five minutes or so. Would that be all, sir?'

Holmes appeared to be oblivious to this question, so I answered on his behalf.

'Five minutes or so ... ha!' Holmes

168

exclaimed mysteriously, once the butler had departed.

By now I could not be sure as to whether it was Hopkins or myself who was the most exasperated.

'Really, Holmes, could you please explain the relevance of your questioning of Archer and your reference to this 'Morgan the Poisoner'? I remember seeing his name in your long list of 'Ms', but other than that I know nothing of the case whatsoever, nor its current relevance,' I complained.

'Inspector, do you remember there being one outstanding and distinguishing feature in the case notes description of Morgan?' Holmes asked excitedly.

'I do, as a matter of fact. He had two fingers missing from his right hand,' Hopkins replied.

'No doubt you have also noticed how Hastings-Thomas habitually keeps his arms crossed in a manner that conceals his right hand?'

'Now that you come to mention it, I had noticed that, and the fact that he puts his hands in his pockets a good deal,' I confirmed.

'Excellent, Watson. In that case you will now appreciate the little experiment that I carried out during our interview with

Hastings-Thomas.'

By way of an explanation, Holmes took out his silver vesta box and went through the motion of hurling it towards my face. Thankfully, on this occasion, he did not release the box. However, my right hand sprang forward instinctively, in an effort to protect my face.

'Good heavens, Holmes!' I exclaimed. 'I presume, therefore, that you were already suspicious of the man.'

'You must have thought my behaviour rather eccentric at the time. However, you forget that there is always an excellent reason behind every one of my actions. Before you ask me, I can confirm that there were two fingers missing from the right hand of Hastings-Thomas!' Holmes dramatically confirmed.

'I congratulate you, Mr Holmes, for you have surely revealed our killer. I shall summon my constables at once!' As Hopkins rose from his chair to set about taking Hastings-Thomas, or perhaps I should now refer to him as Morgan, into custody, Holmes suddenly called him back.

'No, Inspector! It is too early and Morgan could yet slip through our net once again.' Holmes barked out this order somewhat aggressively. However, he soon remembered himself and drew a deep breath, before he smiled at the perplexed Stanley Hopkins.

'I apologize, Inspector. Of course, it is your case and your decision. However, before we commit ourselves it is important that we are satisfied we have the proof to justify his immediate arrest. Everything we have discussed so far would be thrown out of court as being purely circumstantial evidence.'

Hopkins returned slowly to his chair, crestfallen, and resigned to the truth.

'Of course, you are correct, Mr Holmes, in everything that you have said. But we cannot allow a dangerous criminal, like Morgan, to retain his liberty for a moment longer than we have to.'

'I agree with you, Inspector. Yet I am more concerned about what he might do, rather than what he already has done,' Holmes said.

'Whatever do you mean, Holmes?' I asked, feeling more confused than before by my friend's revelation.

'We must consider the fact that Morgan's previous victim was his first wife. Obviously, following the death of her father, it is likely that Julie will come into a considerable sum of money. Under their present circumstances, I think that it is not unlikely that Morgan might be tempted into committing a similar crime and for the same reason.

'This we have to prevent, and yet I am not now convinced that Morgan is Abernetty's murderer. He has gone to great lengths to establish a new identity. Do we honestly think it is likely he would jeopardize that by committing a crime in such an obvious set of circumstances? Every facet of his evidence has been corroborated by others.

'A man of his undoubted intellect would hardly return from a fishing trip and then promptly deliver the very item that he has just poisoned. He has made himself conspicuous with his every word and action. Is that the likely behaviour of a man trying to conceal a crime? Besides, how would he have known about Mrs Abernetty's sleeping draught? Not to mention its exact location. No, I am not now convinced of Morgan's guilt,' Holmes finally admitted.

'If he is not the murderer, then who, in heaven's name, committed the crime? Furthermore, if Morgan is allowed to leave this house, how do we prevent him from committing such a crime at some time in the future?' Hopkins asked, with an air of desperation in both his voice and his manner.

'There may still be a way of answering both your questions, Inspector, although, by the time that moment comes, you might be horrified by the answers,' Holmes replied.

'You are, undoubtedly, referring to the dish of butter that you asked Hopkins to deposit, so ceremoniously, in the pantry, this afternoon,' I ventured.

Holmes nodded emphatically while he put a match to his neglected pipe.

'Once I had established and, perhaps exaggerated, the importance of the dish of butter, it was then important for me to ensure that everybody knew of its location. You paraded it before them so nobly, Inspector, that I was left in little doubt that our murderer would be lured to retrieve the evidence at some point during the night. Now, however, I am not so sure.

'I shall require some stationery and Granville, the page,' Holmes stated simply.

'You have not yet explained the reasons behind your questioning of the butler. For some reason you became excited when you heard that Dr Cardew had only been present for barely five minutes,' I mentioned, on my way over to the bell pull.

Before Holmes had a chance to answer, Archer responded to my call most promptly and Holmes then gave him his instructions. Once the door had closed behind him, Holmes suddenly turned towards me, his elbows perched precariously upon his bony knees.

'Now think, Watson,' Holmes began with some intensity, 'were there any other unusual features on Abernetty's body that you might have overlooked when you examined him earlier?'

Admittedly the evidence of Dr Cardew and my own discovery of the arsenic traces about Abernetty's lips had probably curtailed the thoroughness of my assessment. Consequently, I thought back, long and hard, before I gave Holmes my considered reply.

'I must confess that I overlooked some unusual features of Abernetty's fingers and nails,' I admitted. 'I was so transfixed by the deadly substance around his lips, and in view of the results of Dr Cardew's own examination, that I disregarded them at the time. However, the blue tint at the base of his nails together with some unusual pitting upon their surface should have warned me of the possibility of serious heart disease.'

I must have appeared somewhat crestfallen when I made this declaration, because Holmes immediately smiled at me and exonerated me for having committed this oversight.

'Do not blame yourself, old fellow. Why would you have doubted the diagnosis of a fellow professional? Besides, in the light of the dramatic nature of Abernetty's death, this other discovery of yours would have appeared to have been somewhat irrelevant. However, your revelation has now thrown a completely different light upon the results of our enquiries. Ah, I believe that is the page!' Holmes exclaimed, upon hearing a knock upon the door.

Sure enough, young Granville came bustling through the door, with some paper, envelopes and a pen held out towards Holmes. The page waited patiently while Holmes wrote out a note and, once the envelope was sealed, Holmes handed it over with some deliberation.

'You know where to deliver this?' Holmes asked.

'Oh yes sir, I have run many an errand there in my time,' Granville confirmed.

'Excellent, now take this for your trouble, but under no circumstances are you to dawdle.' Holmes thrust a number of coins into the young man's palm.

'Thank you, sir, I shall run every step of the way!' Granville promised, as he dashed from the room.

We all smiled at the young man's enthusiasm and then I raised a point of concern with my friend.

'I could not have failed to notice that you deliberately refrained from adding your signature to the note.'

'That, old fellow, would surely have negated the intention of my little warning. I have written this note in the guise of an anonymous friend. Unless I have sorely missed the mark, I fully expect us to receive an impromptu, nocturnal guest.' Holmes pulled out his pocket watch and replaced it with the air of one who had been satisfied with his afternoon's work.

'Now, I believe that we should have sufficient time for a pleasant turn about the garden. Please, Watson, not another question. Let us simply enjoy a fine summer's evening. You shall see and hear enough to satisfy your curiosity before the morning, I assure you.'

With that, Holmes lit up a cigarette and led us back out into the gardens. As we stood out there on the immaculate lawns, I noticed how, one by one, the lights were being extinguished around the house. The all-embracing silence of a late summer's evening revealed the otherwise hidden sounds of the garden's inhabitants: a lonely owl penetrated the stillness with his mournful call; a sharp rustle from a gooseberry bush revealed a hedgehog, perhaps searching for his shelter for the night.

Eventually I noticed Sherlock Holmes trying to determine the best vantage point for his night's vigil, one that would afford him a discreet view of the pantry window. He called Hopkins and I to gather closely towards him, as he whispered a stark warning to us both.

'It is absolutely imperative that nobody within the house becomes aware of our covert activities. Upon returning to the house, our behaviour has to appear to be completely normal. The drainpipe, which runs down the wall adjacent to my bedroom window, would seem to be in a decent state of repair and therefore, that is the means by which I shall gain the vantage point of the hedgerow that is closest to the pantry.'

Holmes pointed towards an overgrown clump of bramble and ivy that would conceal him up to the vital moment.

'I know it to be a hardship,' Holmes continued, 'yet I must ask you both to remain vigilant throughout the night. Remain silent, within your respective rooms, but stay alert to every sound and movement that might emanate from the garden below. I will need a witness to everything that might transpire and it is absolutely vital that nobody should reach the garden, other than us. Fail me, gentlemen, and all could be lost!'

Holmes had left us in little doubt that if either Hopkins, or me, fell asleep, it would be nothing less than a fatal error. Therefore, with that in mind, we ordered a further pot of coffee on returning to the drawing-room. As he set the tray down upon the table, Archer informed us that the rest of the household had now retired for the night. He then excused himself to do likewise if there was nothing else that we required.

'Good night, Archer, and thank you. Do not concern yourself, as I will lock the door myself,' Holmes smiled.

Once we had drained the coffee pot and after one last pipe, the three of us silently crept up the stairs and made our way to our respective rooms. I had decided not to get undressed and I took up a position on an uncomfortable, hard-backed chair, that I positioned next to the window. It was only then that I began to regret having left my army revolver behind in its drawer in Baker Street.

Holmes's climb down the drainpipe must have been a silent one. His room was adjacent to my own and I heard not a sound, even when he had opened his bedroom window. The darkness was complete, save for the indigo tint upon the horizon, which is always present at the height of summer.

I strained my eyes to their limit, yet still I could not make out even a indication of Holmes's outline. I only knew of his presence within the undergrowth when I observed the occasional flash of orange flame, which indicated to me the lighting up of yet another cigarette.

I smiled to myself as I considered the number of similar vigils that Holmes had taken up during the course of our long association. I had been a part of many of these and I realized that, on each occasion, I had not been in full possession of the reasons behind them.

For example, I had been completely oblivious to the necessity for the long wait at Stoke Moran until the very moment that Dr Grymsby Roylott had released his murderous snake!

I did not anticipate that the events of the coming night would be in any way as dramatic as that blood-chilling conclusion, yet I felt that I was still as much in the dark as I had been then. I kept myself awake by lighting a succession of cigarettes of my own. I would have betrayed myself by igniting a lamp, so reading was an impossible diversion.

I constantly referred to my pocket watch by the light of a vesta, and became more and more agitated by its slow movement and the increasing heaviness of my eyes. I began to speculate as to who Holmes was anticipating to appear at the pantry window. In heaven's name, it was only five minutes after midnight!

The reason behind Holmes having the butter dish delivered to the pantry had been obvious to me: he wished to prove that the presence of the arsenic in the butter would have prevented it from melting at its natural speed under the glare of the hot afternoon sun. This he would not be able to prove until the sun achieved exactly the same height during the course of the day ahead. The only person that this would perturb would be the murderer.

Of course, whoever that might be would be taking an enormous risk in potentially revealing themselves. If they did not think that it was a gamble that was worth taking, well, then there was a distinct possibility that our ambush would result in abject failure. However, if Holmes was convinced of its viability, then I was, inevitably, his man.

Another cigarette and another glance at my timepiece . . . 1.30! At that moment the owl took up its mournful call once again. Then I made out another orange flame from behind Holmes's sanctuary. How much longer would we have to wait? I began wondering from which direction the butter thief would make his approach.

A moment later this question would be answered! It was only the absolute stillness of the night that rendered the subtle sound which was barely perceptible. It was, beyond a doubt, the slow and guarded opening of a gate at the far edge of the garden lawn. The intruder was pedantic enough to close it, just as cautiously, behind him, and a hint of moonlight revealed a crouched form that began to sidle gradually towards the rear of the house.

Naturally enough, Holmes was immediately alert to this advance and I could see the tip of his cigarette land on the earth as he threw it away from him urgently. This was the moment for me to begin my own silent approach. Mercifully, the hinges on my door were oiled and silent and I crept down the stairs as deftly as I could.

Hopkins was barely a step behind me and we two approached the back door in single file. Holmes was to have his man and his witnesses, it would seem. I had half expected to see the form of the notorious Morgan struggling within Holmes's vice-like grasp. Or perhaps I would see Clarissa Abernetty sobbing helplessly at Holmes's feet.

Holmes was determined to maintain the silence which he had demanded, at all costs. As a consequence, he held his hand quite firmly over the mouth of his captive, until he was satisfied that the struggle was over.

'Stay silent, I beseech you, for there is still a

chance that we might yet be able to do some good,' Holmes whispered urgently into the criminal's ear. A pair of startled eyes darted towards Holmes and the secured head slowly nodded in agreement. The moment of danger had evidently passed and Holmes released his steely grip with a determined smile.

It was only now that Hopkins and I were able to identify the person in Holmes's custody.

'Dr Cardew!' I exclaimed, although I had still been able to maintain my voice in a hoarse whisper.

Holmes cautioned us all by raising his finger to his lips and indicated that we should all make our way towards the potting shed that was positioned at the rear of the garden. Holmes turned earnestly towards Hopkins.

'Are you certain that your men will maintain the security of the house while we are absent?' Despite our current distance from the house, Holmes had barely raised the volume of his voice.

Hopkins nodded his confirmation.

'They are both diligent young men, Mr Holmes, whom I have placed on full alert. No one will be allowed to leave that house without our say-so, I assure you.'

By this time we had reached the door to the shed.

'Excellent, Inspector. In that case we can

make our way inside to hear the doctor's story. I can assure you that it will not be without points of interest. Oh, and, Watson, do not judge your fellow practitioner too harshly until we have heard him out in full,' Holmes added reproachfully.

Evidently Holmes had observed the look of abhorrence upon my face, that I had not been able to conceal.

'That is very kind of you, Mr Holmes; however, I simply must object to being man-handled in such a manner!' Cardew protested. 'Could you now explain to me the meaning behind all this ridiculous skulduggery?'

'Surely the pertinent question should be, why do we find you lurking behind the Abernettys' house in the middle of the night?' Holmes responded.

The doctor blustered and stammered for a moment or two, before voicing his inadequate reply.

'If you must know, this evening I received an anonymous note informing me that it would be to my advantage if I was to examine the butter dish that you had secured within the pantry. My curiosity was certainly aroused by this, so I decided to take the advice of my unknown benefactor.'

'Did you not ask yourself in what way you

might benefit from taking this advice?' I decided to ask.

'Or, did you already know?' Holmes added with a most knowing smile, one that stopped Cardew in his tracks. This time his reply was a silent one and he glared at each one of us in turn, in a state of blind panic.

'Do not distress yourself unduly, Doctor. I believe that I have unravelled the nature of your secret. However, if you supply me with the finer details, and answer me with complete honesty, there might yet be found a satisfactory solution,' Holmes suggested calmly.

Doctor Cardew bowed his head in shame and he then solemnly nodded his head in submission.

'Is that really possible?' he asked pathetically.

'Believe me, Dr Cardew, you would have found yourself in handcuffs by now, and we would be having this conversation within the comfort of the house, if I did not think that it was,' Holmes confirmed, while he indicated that we should now make our way into the shed.

There were several wooden crates strewn about the place, which made for adequate seating, although the lack of light prevented me from making my customary notes. Everything that transpired, amongst the gardening equipment, I relate solely from memory.

I could tell from his steely silence that Inspector Hopkins was uncomfortable with the form of these proceedings. However, he was willing to give Holmes the benefit of the doubt as his previous experience of his method had always proved to be a positive and advantageous one.

'Doctor Cardew, before we listen to your story, I must immediately clear up one area of confusion. Namely, that it was I who sent you the anonymous letter of warning,' Holmes announced.

'You, Mr Holmes?' Cardew exclaimed incredulously. 'Well then, surely you must know it all. There is nothing more that you can learn from me.'

'Undoubtedly I know a good deal, but certainly not all,' Holmes confirmed. 'Perhaps you would be good enough to start at the very beginning and explain to us at which point you first decided to poison Mr Montague Abernetty.' Holmes would never have listed diplomacy amongst the finer facets of his character.

At this juncture Stanley Hopkins decided to offer cigarettes to each of us. Even Dr Cardew took one, reluctantly, and I noticed that his hand was trembling terribly when the flame briefly illuminated it. He coughed uncontrollably for several minutes after his first pull and immediately handed the cigarette back.

'I apologize, gentlemen, but it is probably the wrong time for me to start a new habit.' Once he had calmed himself, Cardew began to tell us of his relationship with Montague Abernetty.

'You must understand, from the beginning, that I was not merely the Abernettys' family doctor. Over the many years of our acquaintance, I had become their closest friend and most trusted adviser. I had even been nominated to act as the executor of their estate in the event of their demise.

'However, it was in my capacity as a doctor that I first became aware of Montague's problems and his unusual solution for them both. Sadly, and ironically, it was the medical problem that I could do the least about solving for him. For many years he had suffered with an irregular heartbeat and a degree of breathlessness. This I had been able to keep under control with medication . . . up to a point. But when this condition gradually deteriorated I realized that Montague would, before very long, require a far greater skill than I was able to provide him. I referred him to an old friend of mine who kept a flourishing practice in Wimpole Street, which specialized in conditions such as his. Unfortunately, my friend's conclusions ran very much upon the same lines as my own had done. Montague would be dead within a few months and the last few weeks of his life would prove to be both painful and distressing. Not just for himself, of course, but also for his beloved and devoted wife, Winifred. You must understand that the motive behind almost every one of his actions was to spare Winifred any unhappiness or anxiety.

'Of course, this he was not always able to do. For example, when his younger daughter, Clarissa, threatened to pull the family apart by persisting with her doomed romance with a philandering artist, it was Montague who instigated their separation by refusing to release Clarissa's dowry until she agreed to break off this most inappropriate of associations. This she refused to do, but when the scoundrel heard of the loss of the dowry he took little time in seeking another source for his finance, leaving Clarissa heartbroken and distraught.

'Montague tried to distance his wife from the grief that these circumstances could have caused her. However, he only achieved in pushing his daughter further away from him and into the reassuring arms of her mother.' Doctor Cardew paused for a moment or two, as he pondered what was to follow.

'I suppose that it was at this moment that the serpent of romance raised its ugly head once more and threatened the happiness of Winifred Abernetty yet again.' I was not surprised at the cynical nature of Holmes's question, as his views upon romance had never been positive ones. I could also sense that he was losing patience with Cardew's hesitant and long-winded narrative.

The doctor of Sandwich nodded his head gravely before he continued.

'Montague had never approved of Julie's marriage to Hastings-Thomas. He disliked his son-in-law's indifferent and cavalier demeanour and the fact that his way of life provided Julie with very few of the things that she had, previously, cherished the most — ' At this moment it was Hopkins who decided to prompt the good doctor.

'Excuse me, sir, but what, exactly, was this way of life, that Mr Abernetty had so disapproved of?'

'Hastings-Thomas was a somewhat reckless and, more often than not, an unsuccessful player of the financial markets. Julie was able to satisfy her opulent and extravagant taste by virtue of his initial success. However, this was only short-lived and it was not long before they were forced to move to a modest home in St John's Wood and their treasured luxuries were gradually repossessed. Their inevitable and incessant entreaties for funds were causing Montague grave concern. So, again, in an effort to spare his wife any further anguish, he sought another means of resolving this crisis.'

'I suppose that it was at this point that the letter arrived,' Holmes announced flamboyantly, while lighting a cigarette. 'Watson, I sincerely hope that your mental notes are as accurate and comprehensive as your written reports.'

'I am certain that the inspector and I will be able to cobble something together that will satisfy you,' I replied, somewhat put out by Holmes's rather offhand manner.

Doctor Cardew was more taken aback by Holmes's reference to the letter than his manner.

'Well, upon my word, Mr Holmes, you seem to know as much, if not more of the matter as I do myself! However, I must confess that it was, indeed, at this moment that the letter arrived and Montague first proposed to me his heinous scheme. Acting without Winfred's knowledge, and in an effort to break up Julie's ill-advised marriage, Montague contacted an old friend and colleague of his at the Home

Office, to see if he could uncover any information that might be used against Hastings-Thomas.

'This fellow at the Home Office, whose identity I cannot reveal to you, was successful in a way that even Montague could not have foreseen. The dread that this discovery instilled in him made him even more determined to be rid of the bounder and as a matter of extreme urgency! Apparently, Hastings-Thomas had been suspected of murdering his first wife by arsenic poisoning some years before and he had only escaped the noose because of a technicality. Montague could see no reason to doubt the information from his friend and he immediately confronted his son-in-law with the letter.

'To his horror and astonishment, Hastings-Thomas just laughed in his face! He also informed him that Julie was so besotted with him that he had felt confident enough to inform her of this incident from the outset of their marriage. To Montague's dismay, she had believed every word of his entreaties of innocence and felt more closely bound to him as a consequence. To make matters worse, Hastings-Thomas even threatened to make the matter known to Winifred unless Montague agreed to pay off some of his gambling debts. Montague felt that he had little choice but to comply. He knew that this news would upset his wife dreadfully, something that he would do absolutely anything to prevent.

'All the while, Montague's heart condition was deteriorating and he knew that it would not be long before he would be powerless to prevent his cowardly son-in-law from embedding his claws into his mourning family. His solution was as shocking as it was logical and, believe me, gentlemen, when I tell you that he was in tears when he asked for my assistance with his plans. He proposed to end his own life before the pain became too awful for him to bear and in a manner that would condemn Hastings-Thomas to a sentence that he so obviously deserved.

'Do not, I beseech you, gentlemen, view me too harshly when I inform you that I agreed to do it! What else could I do? My oldest and dearest friend wished to save his remaining family in the only way that he knew how. It would spare his beloved Winifred the anguish of watching him fade away slowly and painfully. It would spare his elder daughter the threat of a murderous husband. Finally, he reasoned, long overdue justice would prevail. I am certain, Mr Holmes, that were it not for your cleverness, we would have succeeded in all three of our endeavours. Now, though, I face being accused of murder, my medical career lying in ruins. Furthermore, the family that I treasure the most will forever live under the shadow of the threat of Hastings-Thomas.'

At this moment, Cardew finally lost control of his emotions and his head sank down as he tearfully contemplated what he viewed as his abject failure.

'Do not be so hasty in your assumptions, Dr Cardew!' Holmes pronounced surprisingly. 'I thank you for making the affair clear to us, but now I think it best if I explain the remainder to my colleagues. Please correct me if I am mistaken in any of my statements.'

Slowly Cardew raised his head once more and nodded his agreement to Holmes's proposal.

'I shall make this brief, for I am certain much has now become obvious to you both and I do not wish the house to be roused before we make our return. The three endeavours that the good doctor referred to, could only have been achieved in one way. Inspector, to begin with, Dr Cardew is not the murderer of Montague Abernetty.'

'Then who the devil is?' the patient inspector demanded to know.

Holmes raised his finger to beg Hopkins's further indulgence and lit another cigarette.

'Doctor Cardew cannot be the murderer

for the simple reason that Montague Abernetty took his own life, although with the doctor's assistance and support. What other recourse could the distraught patriarch have had? Between the two of them they devised a way of incriminating Morgan that would provide the means, opportunity and motive.'

He turned to the doctor. 'I presume that you have retained the letter that so mysteriously disappeared after Mr Abernetty's death?'

By way of a reply, Cardew struggled in his jacket pocket and hauled out a large blue envelope which he promptly passed over to the inspector's eager hand.

'This is astonishing, I must say!' Hopkins exclaimed.

'What other explanation could there be?' Holmes continued. 'We could not fathom out who had removed the missing dose of sleeping draught, for the simple reason that the doctor here, cleverly withheld it from the last prescription. They knew that by him doing so they were immediately incriminating the person who delivered the tray.

'The doctor quite easily obtained a quantity of arsenic, the poison which they knew Morgan had used to kill his first wife, and Abernetty applied the poison to his own butter. By doing so he felt certain that he would be blasting the plans of his evil and avaricious son-in-law and sparing his poor wife any further anguish. The doctor, here, merely provided the means and now, Inspector, we need you to show similar understanding. After all, are we not here for the same reason? Specifically, that is to see justice served!'

'But why did Dr Cardew come here tonight to retrieve the butter dish?' the bemused inspector asked.

'Simply because my anonymous note warned him, in a friendly tone, that all would be lost if he did not do so. He was most anxious to discover who else knew of his and Abernetty's plans and ensure himself of their silence,' Holmes explained.

'You do realize that you are asking me to arrest and condemn an innocent man based on the word of Dr Cardew and this letter?' Hopkins was clearly greatly troubled by Holmes's outrageous proposal.

'I beg you, Inspector, not to refute the validity of the letter before you have inspected the signature at its base,' Doctor Cardew implored.

Holmes offered Hopkins a match so that he could do so in the dark of the shed.

'Good heavens!' Hopkins exclaimed. 'Why, it is none other than the Home Secretary himself! That does, indeed, throw a different light upon the matter.'

'Inspector, we are all sworn to silence and you will be credited with the arrest of Morgan the Poisoner and the final closure of one of Scotland Yard's more embarrassingly open case files.' Holmes tried one final point of persuasion in a most dramatic and, ultimately successful, fashion.

'Very well,' Hopkins agreed sombrely. 'However, we must repair to the house immediately in order that the deed is done with some discretion. I will also insist that we construct our case in such a manner that Morgan escapes the gallows. I would not sanction his death at my hands under these conditions, but there is no good reason for him to remain a free man if I have the means of removing him from society.'

'Well said, Inspector!' Holmes slapped Hopkins upon his shoulder and then led our small procession from the potting shed and back to the house just as the first light blue glimmer of dawn was creeping above the surrounding tree-line.

For my part, I could still not quite believe what I had just heard and witnessed. The ambiguity of the moral question was one that would take me some time to come to terms with. There was no question that Morgan deserved the justice that was surely coming his way. However, the manner of that being achieved was dubious, to say the least.

Holmes appeared to be satisfied with his night's work and Dr Cardew was certainly a much relieved man. After all, he had been certain that his great friend's plans were to have come to nothing and that he had been in grave danger of losing his own liberty. That was until the intervention of that champion of justice, Mr Sherlock Holmes. At least, on this occasion, I had been able to console myself with the thought that the liberty that Holmes had taken, had been sanctioned by a member of the official force.

Morgan was arrested as he rose for breakfast, with as little fuss as possible, although his protests succeeded in awakening the rest of the house. Julie appeared to be the only person present who regretted Morgan's dramatic removal, yet even she greeted this in the same stoic fashion as she displayed at the death of her father. It would seem that everybody receives the companion that they deserve.

Hopkins followed Morgan and his officers to the local police station once it was agreed that Holmes would help him to prepare the case prior to the trial date.

Rather pointedly, neither Holmes nor I raised the topic of the Abernetty mystery throughout the remainder of our trip and we were greeted with great warmth upon our delayed arrival at the Colliers' delightful shore-side villa. Holmes wished to extend our stay for as long as possible, and he spent endless hours in solitary walks along the sand. The thoughts that he was harbouring, throughout these walks, I could only speculate upon.

It would be several months after our return from the coast, before Morgan was finally convicted and condemned to the gallows for the murder of Mr Montague Abernetty. However, it was only after the conclusion of the trial that it came to light that new evidence had been discovered that would surely have convicted Morgan for the murder of his first wife, had it been known at the time.

Naturally, that would have proved irrelevant as the law forbids a second trial for the same crime. Nevertheless, I could think of at least three people who would be much relieved by this fresh evidence.

For, surely, this was the final vindication of the judgment that had been made that night in the Abernettys' garden.

3

THE ADVENTURE OF
THE RELUCTANT SPIRIT

PART ONE

Mrs Cecil Forrester

Mrs Cecil Forrester is a name that will forever retain a special place within my heart and mind, for it was she who first recommended the services of Sherlock Holmes, to her young governess, Miss Mary Morstan. That first meeting was to lead Holmes and me upon the most singular adventure of the 'Sign of Four'. Furthermore, Mary became my first love and wife as a consequence of that auspicious encounter within the rooms of 221b Baker Street.

Mary's tragic and premature passing is a pain that will, undoubtedly, endure within me until the day that my heart and memory both cease to function. Therefore it was understandably a most poignant moment when a letter arrived for me from the very same lady who had once employed my beloved Mary as her governess.

While it is true to say that I had maintained limited contact with Mrs Forrester and I had even, from time to time, made the journey to her home in Clerkenwell for afternoon tea, I was somewhat surprised to receive her letter so soon after the tragic boating accident that had taken her only daughter, Evangeline, so suddenly from her. The poor woman was now, sadly, alone.

For some reason I felt compelled to leave the envelope unopened for an hour or two, while my memories and feelings were given a chance to subside. Equally, I was in no mood to be lectured by Holmes on the subject of allowing my emotions to obstruct my objectivity. So I thrust the envelope within my breast pocket and decided to let it wait until I could read it within the sanctuary of my own room.

The concealment of the letter could not have been better timed. At that precise moment my friend made his abrupt and impromptu return from an enquiry that had seen him absent from Baker Street for a full three days. His outlandish appearance did not surprise me, for he had employed his disguise as an impoverished street peddler on many a similar occasion. However, I was somewhat taken aback by the manner of his return. It had been through the open back window of the house.

'My dear fellow!' I exclaimed. 'What occurrence could have induced you to return in such a clandestine fashion? Surely your incomparable disguise would have provided you with sufficient security?'

'Well, one would have thought so!' In disgust Holmes threw his wig and his bedraggled greatcoat angrily down onto the floor by the fire, before systematically removing the remainder of his camouflage. His hands were, quite literally, quivering with rage as he attempted to light a cigarette and, once it was alight, Holmes smoked it with a feverish hunger.

Another smoke followed immediately afterwards then Holmes collapsed into his chair and proceeded to strum his fingers upon its arm in a most irritable and irritating fashion.

'My goodness, Holmes, what event could have possibly brought about so ill-tempered and urgent a retreat?' I asked hopefully, for it was quite often at a time of crisis that Holmes would be at his most reticent in presenting the facets of a case to me.

Inevitable silence followed my enquiry and the strumming of his fingers seemed to intensify.

'Assure me, at least, that you have not suffered an injury of any sort,' I persisted.

'The only injury that I have suffered is to my pride, if you must know,' Holmes responded reluctantly.

'Well, I am certainly relieved to learn that, at any rate,' I commented. 'I suppose it is the affair of the Tankerville Club that has so ruffled your feathers.'

'Ha! That trifling affair — I had it wrapped up in a week!' Holmes snapped back. The strumming continued and another cigarette was lit. After another lengthy silence I think that Holmes slowly began to realize that his behaviour was unreasonable and that he owed me some sort of an explanation. He glanced at me furtively from the corner of his eye and emitted a grunt of concession.

'I suppose that you will want to make some notes,' Holmes stated dejectedly and with some resignation.

'Well, of course I do!' I exclaimed excitedly while I dashed over to the desk to retrieve my notebook and pencil.

'Very well then, although I will state initially that neither I, nor the official force, emerges from the affair of the Landsbury sapphire covered with any great distinction. Notwithstanding the unsatisfactory nature of the conclusion of the case, there are some points that may provide a meritorious and scientific study for the more serious students of the art of observation and deduction. That is provided, of course, that you not reduce it to yet another one of your romantic trivializations,' Holmes concluded harshly.

'I feel that I have always done full justice to both you and your method, Holmes. You cannot blame me for attempting to render my writing more palatable to the general public than you might otherwise approve of,' I protested.

'A soufflé is more palatable than a dose of medicine, yet that does not render it as more beneficial to the metabolism. Nevertheless, you may deal with this as you will.

'My suspicion that the disappearance of the Landsbury sapphire would prove to be a case that was out of the ordinary was initially aroused by the fact that it was not brought to my attention by either Scotland Yard or by the Landsburys themselves. I knew that I would be moving in high society when I received a written invitation from Langdale Pike, to take tea with him at the Langham Hotel on Tuesday last.'

I should point out here that Langdale Pike was a contact of Holmes of whom I did not necessarily approve. He was a gossip columnist of the worst type, who would not hesitate to destroy a reputation if he felt that his column would benefit from a damning exposure. He was widely read by those who moved in society and, as a consequence, it was members of their rank who suffered the most at his hands.

Holmes and he had forged an arrangement of exchange, whereby Holmes would supply

Pike with the ammunition that he would then fire off in his column. Meanwhile, Pike, in his turn, provided Holmes with a gateway to polite society and its dark underbelly, access to which Holmes might otherwise have been denied.

The advantageous nature of the information, which he received in such a fashion, seemed to satisfy any potential threat to Holmes's sense of scruples. Nevertheless I retained my own reservations regarding this long standing and dubious arrangement.

Holmes stood up and strode to the window where he lit a cigarette and gazed down upon the thriving thoroughfare below. His sharp profile drew a stark outline against the grey skyline beyond the glass. He did not appear to be as drawn or gaunt as was common with him on the conclusion of one of his more problematic cases. Therefore, I deduced that, perhaps, the affair of the Landsbury sapphire had not been as harrowing as his dramatic reappearance had made it initially seem.

'As Pike came towards me in the tea room, the pomade was positively gleaming upon his opulent head of hair and those extravagant moustaches, to the extent that he almost slithered towards me from his chair. As a consequence, I very nearly recoiled when he offered me his hand. He greeted me with a broad, open smile that exposed his gold tooth and an unlit cigarette protruded from its long ivory holder.

'Once the tea things had been removed, Pike finally put a light to his gaudy protrusion and came straight to the point of the matter. The theft of the sapphire was deemed to be a matter of such great delicacy that the Landsburys refused to bring its appropriation to the attention of the police until they were certain that there was no other recourse open to them. Pike had assured them that I was the only recourse! Sadly for Pike, on this occasion I had no information to exchange for his introduction. However, he laid the facts before me, nonetheless. What knowledge do you have of the Landsbury sapphire?' Holmes suddenly asked of me.

Holmes caught me unawares and I needed to pull upon my pipe before I managed to recall an article in *The Times*, of some months before.

'Lord Hector Landsbury . . . of course! It was he and his team of diggers, who recovered the fabled 'Treasure of Thebes' in '84. As I recall, the sapphire, perhaps the largest that has so far been discovered, is the last item from that treasure to remain in private ownership. The remainder of the haul has been systematically donated to museums and institutions throughout the civilized world.

'The article referred to Landsbury's decision to cut the stone and have it transformed into a set of jewellery for his wife. However, I must confess that I have not subsequently read anywhere of its theft,' I concluded.

Holmes turned away from the window and began to applaud me.

'Bravo, Watson, you have been correct upon every point, save one! The sapphire has, indeed, been stolen and you are now one of only three people, outside of the Landsbury family, who know of its disappearance. There, you will now appreciate, is the wonder of the thing.'

'To consider that a fabulous item such as the sapphire of Thebes could disappear without the breath of a word appearing in any of the papers is almost unthinkable,' I agreed.

'That was precisely the first point that I raised with Langdale Pike,' Holmes said, while finally abandoning his cigarettes for the weightier smoke of his old clay pipe and shag tobacco.

While he had been pacing around, Holmes had been systematically removing the last vestiges of his disguise, which now lay in a disparate pile on the rug in front of the fire. With his pipe fully alight, he fell into his customary chair opposite to my own and resembled his usual self once more.

'Why did the Landsburys consider Langdale Pike to be the only man, other than yourself, to be worthy of their trust?' I asked. 'After all, his business is surely to publicize society scandals, not to suppress them.'

'Believe me, Watson, when I tell you that his silence undoubtedly came at a considerable price. Pike is well known within their circles and once they had sought his advice it did not take him long to inform them of his acquaintance with yours truly. He immediately made an appointment with Lady Landsbury for the following afternoon.'

'I find it most unusual that your interview was arranged with the lady of the house and not Lord Hector himself,' I mentioned.

'Sadly, that intrepid explorer and dedicated philanthropist is now merely a frail shadow of his former self. The ravages of time and persistent illness have rendered him to the point whereby it was felt that this catastrophe would be far too much for him to bear.

'Mercifully, Lady Landsbury is not one for time-consuming niceties and once I had been shown through, she immediately led me to the room in which the jewel had been secured.'

Holmes leapt up from his chair at this point and refilled his pipe from the Persian slipper that sat upon the mantelpiece. He was now clearly warming to his story and was so anxious to continue that he almost choked upon a huge intake of smoke that had not been fully inhaled by the time that he next chose to speak.

'Almost immediately I could see how matters really lay. You purport to know my method, Watson, so I am certain that you will believe me when I tell you that my deductive powers were not to be sorely tested on that particular afternoon. Well, not initially, at any rate.

'Lady Landsbury informed me that the Thebes sapphire had been secured within a false drawer at the base of Lord Hector's office desk. His study was on the uppermost floor and the keys to both the drawer and the door to the study were always kept upon his person. I must tell you that both keys are still to be found attached to Lord Hector's belt.

'Lady Landsbury was surprisingly patient while I made a most thorough examination of the locks to both the desk and the study door. I can assure you, Watson, that my lens revealed not a single scratch or blemish upon either. I then turned my attention to the windows and their sills. I am afraid to say that I provided Lady Landsbury with a considerable scare by the degree that I extended my body through an open window. Obviously I did this in order to establish the plausibility of somebody gaining access to the room through that avenue.

'The climb was a treacherously sheer one, although not an impossibility. However, it is certainly not a climb that I would relish, even allowing for the disregard for my own safety of which you have so often accused me. Be that as it may, Lady Landsbury assured me that unless the room was occupied, the windows were always kept locked and the blinds secured firmly behind them. I could verify this statement for myself, by virtue of the good condition of the sash ropes and the lack of scratches behind the securing pin on the blinds. A casual conversation with one of the footmen confirmed that neither the ropes nor the blinds had been renewed in some considerable time. My examination of the windows did not reveal a single mark or print; so I was now satisfied that nobody had entered the room from that direction either.'

Holmes paused for a moment, while he puffed on his pipe and offered me a cognac from the decanter. I gratefully accepted this, but I could not refrain from expressing both my confusion and curiosity during the brief interval in Holmes's long and, frankly, dry narrative.

'Holmes, you are informing me of a crime that appears to have been impossible to commit. You tell me of a precious stone that was taken from a room, but it is a room that, apparently, nobody had been able to gain access to!' I exclaimed in a state of some exasperation.

Holmes eyed me disparagingly for a moment or two, before making his, inevitably, condescending reply.

'Oh, Watson, you have surely eliminated the impossible and yet you have failed to speculate upon the improbable. Do you not find any of my findings in the least bit suggestive?'

'Well, I suppose that they throw up two distinct possibilities,' I began tentatively. 'Either the theft was carried out by someone who had access to both the key to the study and the one that opened the desk drawer, or, otherwise, it would mean that the jewel had not been there in the first place.'

Holmes clapped his hands together and seemed to be delighted by my reply.

'Exactly, Watson, they both appear to be improbable and yet one of them had to be the solution. Once I had decided to grant Lady Landsbury the benefit of the doubt, I had to inform her that a member of her own household must have been the perpetrator of the theft. Assuming that none of the servants would have even known of the existence of the keys, much less their significance and location, I had to inform her that, in my opinion, one of her three sons had to have been the guilty party.

'Mercifully, I was spared the shrill hysterics that might well have resulted from her receiving this appalling news. Instead she sat down slowly and stared forlornly in front of her whilst maintaining a stoic silence. Then she shook her head slowly, from side to side, as she repeated the name of Michael, over and over again. It transpires that Michael is the name of her eldest son and a man who is constantly getting himself into one financial scrape or another. Then, it occurred to me that a man of his background and upbringing would have found it impossible to dispose of a prize as famous and valuable as the Thebes sapphire. Perhaps there was another motive behind the jewel's disappearance.'

'Was it mere coincidence that the sapphire happened to disappear only a short time after it had been announced that Sir Hector intended to have it cut at last?' I speculated.

'That is precisely the question that I began to ask myself,' Holmes confirmed. 'There had to be a connection between the two occurrences and one that would have prohibited Lady Landsbury from calling in the official force. I decided that I needed to speak to her eldest son, as a matter of urgency. However, I soon discovered that this would not be an easy matter to arrange. Apparently he had not been seen at home for the past two and a half days and there was no way of knowing when he might next return.'

'Well, that is pretty damning, in itself, is it not?' I asked.

'One would have thought so, but then Lady Landsbury reluctantly informed me that her son's disappearance was not as uncommon an occurrence as one would suppose. It was with the greatest reluctance that she informed me that Michael is a member of the notorious Prometheus Club! And it is not unusual for him to remain locked within the card-room, at that establishment of ill-repute, for several days at a time. Poker, apparently, is his preferred game and he always emerges drained and considerably poorer.' Holmes paused for a moment, as he drained his glass of its cognac.

I blew a long, low whistle at the mere mention of the name of Michael's preferred club. The Prometheus had accrued a most infamous reputation built upon the hedonistic lifestyle enjoyed by many of its members. Gambling at cards, it had to be said, was amongst the least licentious pastimes enjoyed by its regulars.

'The young man must enjoy a most lucrative career if he is able to maintain membership at a club such as that one,' I commented.

'Ah, now we come to the crux of the matter. Watson, the young man has never done a day's work in his life! The price of his membership and the repayment of the huge debts that he has subsequently accrued have all been funded by his family. I can assure you that this has come at a considerable and financially crippling cost.

'Despite all my efforts, Lady Landsbury strenuously and repeatedly denied that she was withholding any other information that might aid me in my enquiry. She only discovered the jewel's theft because she had decided to take one last look at that remarkable treasure before it was cut up, and that she could add nothing further to what I already knew.

'Therefore, in my guise of the old peddler, I decided to mount a protracted vigil outside the Prometheus Club, until such time as Michael Landsbury finally decided that the cards had won the day. Armed with a small photograph of her son with which Lady Landsbury had supplied me, I took up a position in a sheltered alleyway, which lay barely ten feet away from the entrance to the club. This was at eleven o'clock in the evening and my quarry did not resurface until three o'clock the following afternoon.'

'Good heavens, Holmes you must have been exhausted!' I exclaimed sympathetically.

'Be that as it may, I was not nearly as fatigued as young Landsbury appeared to be. I observed him repeatedly rubbing his dark, bloodshot eyes as he tried to readjust to the light outside of the club. He could barely stand up, much less attempt to walk anywhere, and I observed him as he tried repeatedly to summon a cab, without enjoying any success. This, I now decided, was the moment for me to intervene and I shuffled over to him, from my alleyway.'

'Why did you decide to intercept him in the guise of the old peddler instead of as your own person?' I then asked him.

'I would surely have drawn more attention to myself had I done so. An elderly peddler would not look so out of place as me, in such a situation and for so long a period of time. Besides which, I did not wish to intimidate him before I had a chance to let him know how matters really stood.' Holmes paused for a moment, to light his pipe once more.

'Now I understand; our back streets and

alleys are sadly teeming with poor souls such as your peddler.' Holmes ignored my comment and resumed his most singular story without a moment's delay.

'Landsbury barely gave me a glance as I approached him, and I immediately began begging for a penny or two in the most heart-rending voice that I could muster. He must have endured the most appalling luck at the tables, as he dismissed my plea for alms without a moment's hesitation. He was too much of a gentleman to manhandle me from his presence, but he soon resumed his search for a hansom, even while I was tugging on his sleeve. Just when it seemed that his search for transport was about to end, I suddenly pulled up to my full height and addressed him by name and in my normal tone of voice.

'The transformation that now overtook him was as astonishing as it was instantaneous. The strain of losing at cards over a three-day period, coupled with my abrupt metamorphosis, were too much for the young fellow to cope with and he fainted away into my arms.

'The moment of the cab's arrival could not have been better timed. The driver obligingly dropped down to help me haul Landsbury into his vehicle. Subsequently we circled the surrounding streets for an hour or two while Landsbury slowly recovered and gave me his version of the Thebes sapphire affair.'

'Do you mean to say that you actually sat there talking to a man who had stolen from his own family? Surely you should have delivered him directly to Scotland Yard!' I exclaimed, aghast at my friend's apparent indifference to Landsbury's crime

'Watson, you seem to have forgotten the promise that I had given to Landsbury's mother. Besides, I was already convinced that the impending dissection of the jewel was the reason behind its theft in the first place. Do not mistake my willingness to hear his account of things as mere apathy on my part. Open your mind and view the known facts from a different perspective,' Holmes suggested provocatively.

Before replying, I slowly lit up a pipe of my own and then reappraised everything that I had just heard from Holmes. The circumstances of the theft, the reason behind it and its timing, all seemed to point towards the same inevitable conclusion. However, if Landsbury had been unable to realize the value of the stone, what other motive could he have had for betraying his family?

I raised this point with Holmes, and immediately my question was greeted with a broad smile of satisfaction.

'So, Watson, you have finally learnt how to

ask the correct questions. We have already deduced that Michael Landsbury was the perpetrator of the theft. However, we have also assumed that his motive was based entirely upon greed and selfishness. The timing of the theft is the key, Watson.'

'Perhaps he knew something about the stone that he did not wish to be discovered when it was finally sent to be cut. Could it have been a fake?' I asked, but with very little conviction.

'Oh, Watson, you have simply excelled this time! In a strange way Michael seemed to be relieved when I put the very same question to him in the cab. It was as if the act of confession would now remove the huge burden that had been sitting for so long upon his back. Once I had received that reaction from him, it did not take me long to extract the entire story.

'Once his mother had realized that her husband's descent into illness was one from which he would not be climbing back, she decided to take steps that would provide for the future well-being of her family. Moreover, Michael's constant demands for money had been driving the Landsburys towards financial ruination. Her last and only resort proved to be the sale of the Thebes sapphire.

'Using Langdale Pike as an intermediary,

she arranged a clandestine sale to an eminent and extremely wealthy Egyptologist, who was willing to pay a price which was way above the auction value for this legendary acquisition. Rather cleverly she had a worthless replacement made that would satisfy any curious observer should they ask to view the famous stone. All the while she decided to maintain the sapphire's original insurance. Of course, she did not realize that she had been overheard whilst she was engaged in these dubious arrangements — '

'By her son, Michael . . . of course!' I exclaimed excitedly.

'The remainder, I am sure, you can conclude for yourself,' Holmes assumed correctly.

'I have surely misjudged that young man. He has sacrificed himself for the sake of his family's honour. He stole the stone to save his mother from the shame of having the fake being discovered by her husband's jeweller and, of course, by the insurers who will now suffer a huge loss — provided that the whereabouts of the stone remain a mystery, I would assume.' I let out a long, low whistle when I considered the potential insured value of such a glorious prize.

'Watson, let us not forget that Michael's behaviour and character are not entirely without blemish. It was his addiction that created his family's problems in the first place. However, he now realizes that the police will have to be referred to the case if the insurance is to have any validity, and that flight is now, therefore, his only option.'

Holmes could obviously sense my forthcoming objection and tried his best to appease me.

'Do not concern yourself, Watson. Although I have now referred the case to our old friend Inspector Lestrade, I have also promised Michael twenty-four hour's grace to escape, before I give Lestrade the help that he will so surely require. I will certainly enjoy the spectacle of Lestrade chasing his own tail while Michael Landsbury sets forth to seek his fortune in India.

'I should be very much surprised if we were to hear any further news of that young man and I sincerely hope that his redemption has now been duly realized. As for Lady Landsbury, well, I trust that it will not be long before she receives the insurance funds that she so sorely needs and that she will then accept the fact that her eldest son has vindicated himself at last.'

'You have certainly resolved the matter in a way that is satisfactory for all concerned, save for Inspector Lestrade, of course. Yet you have still not adequately explained the reason for your impromptu and unconventional return to our rooms a while earlier,' I now asked, although I was still not certain that the moral issue of Michael's escape was sitting that easily with me.

Holmes's entire demeanour altered as I asked for this explanation. He lit a cigarette and turned away from me, as though attempting to avoid my curious gaze.

'The manner of my return had nothing whatsoever to do with the Thebes sapphire affair, I assure you, Watson. However, I am afraid that your avaricious readers will have to wait for some considerable time before I am at liberty to reveal the details of that particular case and allow them to be condemned to their inevitable fate within the bowels of your dreaded notebook!

'But see, you might yet have something of far more interest hidden there in your jacket pocket.' Holmes had evidently observed a corner of Mrs Forrester's letter protruding from my inside breast pocket and he was now pointing towards it excitedly.

I laughed, once I realized that Holmes was expecting to discover a stimulating case from within the letters of my old friend.

'I am certain that you will not find anything of interest in here,' I said, as I removed that long forgotten piece of correspondence. I decided to excuse myself so that I might read this reminder of my past within the confines of my own room.

'By all means, my dear fellow,' Holmes acceded, no doubt recalling the significance of the name of my correspondent and, therefore, the potentially personal nature of the letter's contents.

I turned up an oil lamp that sat on my table by the window and poured myself a small sherry before I began to read. Initially I was considerably relieved as soon as I realized that, on this occasion at least, Mrs Forrester had no intention of bringing up the subject of my poor, dear Mary. The memory of her was still too painful for me to bear and I was grateful for the omission. However, as I began to read on, I soon understood that Holmes's vision of the letter was going to prove to be closer to reality than my own had been.

Her daughter, Evangeline, had tragically died as a result of a boating accident, on a river near Oxford. The loss of a child is the hardest loss to bear, but, as Evangeline was an only child, for Mrs Forrester it also meant that she would now have to see out her remaining years in solitary desolation. I decided there and then, that I would become a more frequent correspondent and visitor than I had been so far.

Then the mood of the letter dramatically shifted and changed. Had her tragic loss somehow caused Mrs Forrester to lose her grasp of reality? Was this the same woman who had taken such a keen and intelligent interest in the affair of 'The Sign of Four', when I had visited Mary at their home in Clerkenwell?

Apparently, Mrs Forrester had struck up an acquaintanceship with the infamous Fox sisters during the course of her extended visit to New England just a few years earlier. The Fox sisters had earned themselves quite a reputation for having conducted a series of very 'successful' séances and they were now at the very forefront of the fashionable spiritualist movement that was gathering apace on both sides of the Atlantic.

Mrs Forrester had attended one such event and had become so overwhelmed and affected by the events that she had witnessed, that she decided to attempt to invoke the spirit of Evangeline by similar means. The Fox sisters had recommended to her a widely respected medium, one Joseph Carlisle, who also happened to be a senior member of the London Spiritualists Temple.

Up to this point Mrs Forrester had been let down and disillusioned by a number of fraudsters and charlatans who were preying upon the frail and despairing believers in ever increasing numbers. However, Carlisle had built himself a reputation for both success and, more importantly, integrity, and Mrs Forrester decided to make one final attempt at making contact with her daughter through the powers of Joseph Carlisle.

Carlisle had suggested a series of small and intimate séances as a means of making an initial contact with Evangeline, before attempting a full, visual manifestation. However, Mrs Forrester was already having certain misgivings, not the least of which were Carlisle's frequent requests for donations to the Temple that he was so closely involved with.

Therefore, she requested that Holmes and I might pay her a visit and perhaps provide her with the support and advice that she so obviously required. I immediately snatched up the letter and tore along to present it for Holmes's urgent attention.

He did not appear to be particularly enthused by the abrupt nature of my intrusion. He sat bolt upright by the fire with a lit pipe smouldering between his clenched teeth, before reading through the letter carefully and impassively.

He slapped the sheets of paper with the back of his left hand as an indication of his displeasure at their contents.

'It is an absolute scandal!' he complained vigorously. 'This Carlisle fellow is just the tip of the iceberg, you know. Spiritualism is a social fad of the worst kind and these mediums are merely preying upon the misfortunes of the weak. The time that I once spent with the Dalai Lama threw open a new road to me, and I discovered that it is through meditation that one can realize and recognize our true selves. That is true spiritualism, whereas these séances are nothing more than a dangerous form of theatrics. You must warn your friend and prevent her from starting along so hazardous a path. It can only result in ruination and despair. You must go to her at once!' Holmes suggested dramatically.

'Will you not accompany me to Clerkenwell?' I asked, with some surprise.

'Watson, you seem to forget that the majority of the work that I do has, at its core, solid facts and pure logic. The material world is complex enough without our muddying the waters still further with the introduction of the paranormal.

'No, I shall leave this consultation in your very capable hands, Watson. Besides, I am sure that you and Mrs Forrester will have much to discuss of a more personal nature and the matter is a simple enough one. You must dissuade your friend from taking the path to delusion. Believe me, there are enough wonders all around us without our having to sit together with joined hands and shake a table in an attempt at creating some more.'

Holmes was clearly sceptical upon the subject, almost to the point of ridicule. However, I was resolved to remain open minded on the subject and I would offer my old friend both my advice and my support. When I voiced these thoughts to Holmes he merely shrugged his shoulders and he lit his pipe.

'I suppose that you will have gone out again before my return,' I speculated. 'Presumably by the same means as when you made your entrance earlier?'

'Very likely so.' Holmes smiled, knowing full well that I was trying to extract more details from him regarding his current case. We both knew that my thinly veiled attempts were destined to be futile and I went in search of a cab.

I spent the entire journey to Clerkenwell agonizing over what I was going to discover upon my arrival there. Mrs Forrester's elegant town house remained as I had remembered it, well maintained and neatly painted. When Nancy, the maid, opened the door to me, I was immediately struck by the strong smell of bees wax and lavender by which I had always been affected on each of my previous visits. Despite these familiar effects upon my senses, the atmosphere of profound melancholy that now shrouded the entire building left me with the feeling that I was entering the home of a stranger. Nancy's strained smile of greeting made me feel uneasy and the considerable time that it took for Mrs Forrester to join me in the parlour was disturbing.

When she did finally enter the room, I was shocked and dismayed by the effect that the loss of her daughter had had upon her health and appearance. Obviously, I kept these thoughts very much to myself as I jumped out of my chair to meet her at the door. She placed a frail and shuddering hand upon my shoulder for support and I led her to a chair by the small, flickering fire.

'Oh, John, it is so good of you to answer my plea so promptly. However, I see that your friend Mr Holmes could not be persuaded into taking an interest in an old lady's fanciful whims,' she said, in a voice so frail that I could hardly recognize it.

'He is taking a keen interest in your dilemma,' I lied. 'However, he is currently engaged in an international affair of the utmost moment, one that will not brook even an instant's delay. Rest assured that I shall seek his advice when I next see him.' I could not bring myself to relay to her the tone of Holmes's cynical response and I did not really see the need to.

She seemed to be satisfied with my assurance and, when she asked Nancy to bring us some tea, it was with a more cheerful resolve. We were beginning to stir our cups when Nancy suddenly returned to the room and announced the impromptu arrival of none other than Joseph Carlisle himself!

My hostess appeared to be as surprised by this visit as I was. She asked Nancy to show him through and then immediately despatched her for another cup. I was not really prepared for so early a confrontation with the ardent spiritualist and I was on the point of proposing my early departure, when he burst suddenly into the room.

I was immediately struck by two things. Firstly, that the man's appearance was totally at variance to the one that I had been expecting. Instead of a conniving charlatan standing there before me, I found myself sitting opposite to the very epitome of a professor of science. His strange spindly form was clothed in an ill-fitting Donegal tweed suit that had clearly seen better days. He was quite bald, save for a solitary, defiant tuft of light brown hair that clung precariously to the crest of his long forehead. Furthermore, his absurdly small nose balanced upon it a pair of thin-rimmed metal spectacles through which he squinted with some effort. When he smiled he revealed a set of grotesquely misshapen yellow teeth and breath that could at best be described as toxic.

Yet, despite these obvious physical disadvantages, when he spoke it was with a voice that was both modulated and educated and, despite my unwillingness, I found that it was at once soothing and hypnotic. I received his hand with some hesitancy and reluctance.

I was equally struck by the immediate effect that his presence had had upon the behaviour of Mrs Forrester. She became quite excited and overly attentive in equal measure and I could sense an air of desperation in her reaction to him. It was as if she was convinced that Carlisle now represented her last and only link with Evangeline. She was determined to cling to this connection by any means that she was able. This was despite the fact that Carlisle had so far failed to bring Mrs Forrester any closer to her dead daughter than she had been, prior to his first consultation.

'It is a rare privilege to be able to meet a celebrated adventurer and so respected a chronicler, such as you, Dr Watson. It is such a pity that your colleague, Mr Sherlock Holmes, was not also able to attend our small gathering. I am certain that he would have found it of some little passing interest.' The inside of Carlisle's noxious mouth was, unfortunately, left exposed once more.

'I am certain that he would have done so under normal circumstances,' I agreed. 'However he is, at present, engaged by the Foreign Office upon a matter of the utmost moment. As I understand it, any delay on Holmes's part could well result in the direst international consequences.'

'Of course, I quite understand. No doubt we shall read about these events in one of your forthcoming journals,' Carlisle suggested.

'Due to their highly confidential nature, I would very much doubt that you will.' Then I considered one of Carlisle's previous statements.

'You used the phrase, 'our small gathering', earlier, as if our coming together today was some kind of prearranged event. I can assure you, Mr Carlisle, that my being here on this occasion is due to nothing more than an impulsive and long overdue visit in response to a letter from an old friend,' I explained.

'No doubt, no doubt. However, the reasons

for your being here do nothing to diminish the fact that I consider today to be a most auspicious one. The fact that you are present only goes to confirm those instincts of mine.' Once again I was treated to his lethal smile!

'In what context do you use the word auspicious?' I asked.

'Oh, Dr Watson, I do feel a little anxiety within you. You must not be alarmed, you know, for no harm will befall any of us, I can assure you. Today is indeed auspicious for I feel that the spirit world is both active and extremely vibrant. Your being here merely confirms the feeling I have that we can achieve a material contact with the wandering spirit of Evangeline Forrester on this very day!'

Carlisle annoyed me with his presumption. He made this last statement of his in the tone of a pronouncement of fact, whereas even the existence of spirits is a matter very much open to speculation, much less his expectation of making contact with one! The wounds of her horrendous loss were still very raw and I was aghast at the thought of how Mrs Forrester would respond to what was the potentially false hope of seeing her daughter once again.

The poor woman immediately reacted to Carlisle's announcement in the manner that he had hoped for and expected and the one that I had dreaded the most. I could not be sure if the tears rolling down her cheeks were tears of joy, or whether they had been caused by her inability to accept her daughter's tragic demise. In any event, I was not prepared to see my friend reduced to this sorry pass and so I asked her odious visitor if he would return on another occasion. I reasoned that perhaps, by that time, her emotions would be more stable and, therefore, better able to withstand the attack that Carlisle's notions and practices might subject them to.

As soon as I had voiced this proposal, Carlisle turned to his hostess for confirmation that it was also her desire and intention that he should beat a hasty retreat. Judging by her facial reaction, clearly that was not the case. In fact, she was absolutely aghast at the very idea and chastised me for being so 'stodgy'.

These, then, were the circumstances under which I had decided to participate in my first séance.

I apologized for my initial reluctance to co-operate and begged a moment or two that I might smoke a pipe outside. Mrs Forrester's parlour had suddenly become most claustrophobic for me and it felt good to be in the fresh air once more. As I smoked, I considered my motives for involving myself in the forthcoming ritual.

Assuredly, I did not wish to disappoint my elderly and ailing friend. She was clearly harbouring her own doubts as to the authenticity of Carlisle's powers and his promises of success, so she was, therefore, sorely in need of my support. For her sake I determined to maintain an open mind regarding the proceedings, but was I also attending as a means of satisfying my own morbid curiosity? I could not be certain. However, I was sure that I had now been outside for a longer time than I had originally intended and I did not wish to make Mrs Forrester any more anxious than she already was. I emptied my pipe and returned to her parlour at once.

I was immediately struck by the startling transformation that had taken place within the small room during the course of my relatively brief absence. The thick curtains had been fully drawn and the room would have been engulfed in absolute darkness were it not for a low-flamed oil lamp that had been positioned in the corner furthest from the small circular table.

The tiny flame flickered and shimmered at even the slightest of movements, and this faint orange glow barely tinted the outline of the round wooden table which had been moved to the centre of the floor and four small chairs now carefully spaced around its perimeter.

Evidently, Nancy had been persuaded to join us; however, the weak and shadowy radiance from the lamp in the corner made it impossible for me to tell whether her inclusion had been a voluntary decision or not. In common with the rest of us, Nancy's features were now rendered as nothing more tangible than a vague, sepia impression.

When everything had been positioned to Carlisle's satisfaction, he invited us all to take a seat around the table. He was to sit opposite to me with the ladies on either side of us. We were then asked to grasp the hands of the two people next to us, and to remain quite still while making sure that our eyes remained tightly shut throughout the forthcoming proceedings. Before I closed mine I was determined to ensure that Carlisle's hands were firmly clasped around those of the two women. Surely they would be able to determine whether they remained there during the entire demonstration? I was, therefore, satisfied that any form of physical subterfuge, on Carlisle's part, would now be impossible.

The last thing that I saw before I followed his instruction, was the bizarre sight of

Carlisle throwing his head back and rolling his eyes to the top of their sockets. Even in this singular, unearthly light, the whites of his eyes seemed to gleam back into the room. Carlisle was evidently inducing a form of trance and we sat there, in complete and enrapt silence, while the medium's breathing became progressively heavier and more audible.

I noticed the contrast between the two hands that I was holding on to so tightly. Nancy's were absurdly small and probably smoother than those of a young child. Mrs Forrester's, in sharp contrast, were larger than the average woman's and her spindly fingers were severely crooked and possessed the texture of antique leather. Both hands did share one feature, however: they were both shaking uncontrollably, either through excitement or, perhaps, even sheer fear!

That emotion would have been entirely understandable. Carlisle's breathing was becoming increasingly bizarre and disturbing. Then he began calling out to the spirits which, he maintained afterwards, were floating all around him. To my surprise, he asked them not to be afraid of coming forward and he almost demanded that they should provide us with a sign of their presence.

His naked head, shrouded in the luminous glow from the lamp, was still thrown back and his spectacles slithered from his face and fell onto the floor by his feet. He made no effort to retrieve them and continued with his outlandish chanting.

Then, and without warning, the chanting suddenly stopped and he sat bolt upright as if he had just received a bad shock. I opened my eyes indiscernibly for a second; his eyes reverted to their more natural position, although they were now staring starkly in front of him, as if he was looking, but without seeing. I had not observed it before, but I noticed that there was a small glass tumbler, positioned upside down in the centre of the table.

Carlisle invited the spirits to confirm their presence by moving the glass. I risked disturbing the ambience of the séance by opening my eyes again to confirm that Carlisle's hands were still locked within those of the women. As soon as I was certain that they were, I closed my eyes once more and found myself awaiting a movement from the glass.

Carlisle was undoubtedly a most clever practitioner. I had become as enthralled and as expectant as had my hostess. The combined effects of both the subdued lighting and Carlisle's almost hypnotic voice were most persuasive.

'Come, you spirits. I feel your presence, right here within this small room. Please provide us with the sign that I have asked of you. Be not afraid, for we mean you no harm.' Carlisle repeated his invitation, many times over, in a most lyrical fashion and with each repetition the volume of his voice increased.

I could feel Mrs Forrester become more and more agitated, as each one of Carlisle's calls resulted in failure. Her hand became cold and clammy and the quivering of her fingers, which I had observed earlier, now seemed to be intensifying. I was on the point of suggesting that we abandon the entire fruitless quest, when I heard a sound that I really had not expected.

I dared not open my eyes as I did not want to agitate Mrs Forrester by breaking the circle. However, the sound of a glass moving slowly around the table was unmistakable. It seemed to be making small circular motions close to the middle of the table and gradually, as its velocity increased, the tension around the table became almost excruciating.

'Oh, thank you, spirits, for marking your presence here so clearly. Please tap the glass on the table twice if there is more than one of you here. I am certain that there are. Just two sharp knocks, please, to let us know that you are many.' Carlisle's voice remained surprisingly calm and level throughout the entire proceedings.

Without a moment's hesitation, the response that Carlisle had asked for could be clearly heard. The glass rapped upon the table once and then again, sharply and unmistakably. Evidently there was more than one spirit within the room and, as if to confirm this, the base of the table began to rock from foot to foot.

I could feel the grip of my friend's hand suddenly tighten upon mine, and the unusual uncertainty that was now evident in Carlisle's voice made it appear as if he had not expected this further and more dramatic answer to his pleas any more than the rest of us had.

'Oh, spirits, you are indeed many. Tell me, I implore you, if Evangeline is there with you. Just tap the glass three times upon the table if she is. Simply tap the glass three times if Evangeline is amongst you,' he repeated intensely.

Sure enough, within a minute of his request, Carlisle received the answer that he had been hoping for. There was a most anxious delay between the second tap and the third and its implications were almost too much for Mrs Forrester to bear.

'Oh, Evangeline, is that really you?' she

called out, in a voice that was as anxious as it was happy, a voice that was as full of joy as it was full of tears.

The glass rapped three times more, although now in a far more rapid succession. Carlisle now became concerned that Mrs Forrester's reaction to her emotions might result in her breaking the circle. In a calm but, strangely, authoritative manner, Carlisle spoke to the spirits once again.

'There are so many different voices in my head, so many of you. Please be still that I might speak to Evangeline. Your mother is here with me. She is desperate to be with you again. Please speak to me, Evangeline.' He let out a small cry of desperation, as if the effort of shutting out the unwanted voices was causing him intense pain.

'Oh, Mr Carlisle, what is she saying to you?' Mrs Forrester called out emotionally. 'What is Evangeline saying to you and why can I not speak to her?'

Carlisle seemed not to be aware of anything other than the voices in his head and, instead of responding to Mrs Forrester's questions, he continued to encourage Evangeline to speak to him. All the while he remained within his trance-like state and his calls to the spirits almost resembled a mantra. This only added to the intensity of the moment and

Mrs Forrester's distress now reached a most alarming level.

Mercifully, it was Nancy who broke the chain when her head suddenly jerked forward and she passed out, with her head face down upon the table. Obviously my priority was the health and well-being of the young maid. However, once I had brought her round with some of my salts and satisfied myself that no harm had been done, I turned my attention toward the conductor of this bizarre, disturbing ritual.

Carlisle appeared to be unconscious himself and he was now sunk back in his chair in a state of complete nervous exhaustion. I instructed Nancy to turn the gaslight full on and I bent over to examine the medium. He had gone as white as a sheet and had broken out in a sickly, cold perspiration. My salts were equally effective on Carlisle and he soon began to complain about how close he had been to making a strong physical contact with Evangeline.

Nancy seemed to be aggrieved at having been the one to have broken the chain. However, I consoled her with the thought that the interruption had been a most timely one, for matters had probably gone as far as it was safe for them to go. Mrs Forrester was not to be so easily consoled.

She had been distraught enough before when she had become convinced that she was on the verge of making contact with her tragically lost daughter, however, now that this ecstatic moment had been taken away from her, she became implacable.

She demanded that Carlisle recommence at once before it was too late. He slowly shook his head.

'My dear Mrs Forrester, I assure you that the moment has been lost, albeit temporarily. Besides which, it will take a good forty-eight hours before I am fully recovered from this ordeal. At the end of that time, I assure you that I will be able to bring you and Evangeline back together again, for a little while at least.'

'Oh, I do hope so, Mr Carlisle. Do you really think that it is possible?' Mrs Forrester asked desperately.

Carlisle nodded his head emphatically.

'Absolutely I do. We were so close tonight that I am certain that Evangeline will want to return to establish contact once again. Just allow me those forty-eight hours, please.'

'Oh, I really do not know what to think. What is your view of things, John?' Mrs Forrester turned her attention towards me and I felt three pairs of eyes studying my reaction with uncomfortable intensity. My views of the meaning behind the afternoon's overwhelming experience were tainted with uncertainty.

Carlisle appeared to be mildly amused by my nervous discomfort. He leant forward in his chair and insisted upon a response to Mrs Forrester's question.

'Oh yes indeed, Doctor, you really must let us know if the events that you have just witnessed have done anything to dissipate the air of cynicism that surrounded you when we first sat down around the table.'

I could not tell, from the tone of voice, as to whether his was a genuine desire to know my opinion. On the other hand, if he was anticipating that my endorsement of his success in contacting the spirit world would strengthen his hold over Mrs Forrester, then he was not to be disappointed. Despite my better judgement I found myself admitting that the experience that we had all just shared appeared to have been a genuine one.

In all honesty, I was not able to conceive of any other explanation for all of the facts. I was convinced that Carlisle's hands had not once released their grasp upon the hands of the two women and yet the glass upon the table had moved repeatedly and in accordance with Carlisle's comprehensive instructions.

They all appeared to be surprisingly

relieved to hear my endorsement and Mrs Forrester squeezed my hand for comforting confirmation of my sincerity. It was agreed that I would attend the house again in forty-eight hours' time. Carlisle was convinced that by that time he would be able to satisfy Mrs Forrester's desire to establish physical contact with Evangeline.

My only reservation was provoked by the sight of Mrs Forrester standing guardedly over her desk while she wrote out a cheque for the avaricious Joseph Carlisle. The look of satisfaction upon his most singular face, as he hungrily thrust the cheque into his inside pocket, was disquieting to say the very least.

I was beset by this feeling of unease throughout the entire return journey to Baker Street, and I was looking forward to describing the events in Clerkenwell to my friend Sherlock Holmes, in the hope that his logical interpretation of them would help me to calm my nerves. Of course, I was in little doubt that his current case would preclude his presence at Baker Street for some little time and I therefore took the seventeen steps up to our rooms slowly, and one at a time, in anticipation of his absence.

PART TWO

Mr Langdale Pike

To my great and pleasant surprise, not only was Holmes waiting there for me, but he was stretched out languidly upon his favourite chair with his feet almost touching the fire. Even though his eyes were closed, the smile of contentment upon his face told me that he was not asleep and that his latest case had been resolved to his complete satisfaction. His pose reminded me of a hunter who had just returned from an expedition with a bursting bag of game. All that was missing from this tableau were the dog by his feet and a smouldering gun by his side.

'Well, I must say, Holmes, that I did not expect to find you here in such an attitude. I presume that your current project was concluded prematurely?'

'You presume correctly, Watson,' Holmes replied smugly, although his eyes remained closed while he did so.

I was not certain that this was now an appropriate moment for me to broach the subject of Mrs Forrester's dilemma. Consequently, I hesitated by the door, until Holmes opened his left eye and observed my obvious discomfort.

'Watson, I assure you that the circumstances of my recent case have not changed. Therefore, it would be imprudent for me to divulge any of its details until such time as my brother, Mycroft, so allows.' Holmes obviously assumed that my hesitancy was due to my enduring curiosity as to the conclusion of his mysterious problem.

'I did not realize that your brother was involved. However, that does explain the magnitude and significance of the matter. I presume a grave international dilemma was at the centre of the thing?' I asked.

'I cannot deny it, Doctor. I can assure you of one thing, however, without a risk of betraying my brother's trust: these are dangerous and volatile times for continental Europe, and the consequence of the successful conclusion of this case is that we can all sleep more safely and securely within our beds tonight than might otherwise have been the case,' Holmes concluded gravely.

I slowly shook my head as I contemplated how unpredictable our continued safe existence truly was nowadays.

'My, my, it is hard to appreciate the size of the debt that I, and the public at large, owe to the two Holmes brothers and their cleverness,' I said. Holmes waved this compliment away with aplomb and he turned around towards me and granted me his full attention.

'I perceive that there is another matter that is still troubling my old friend. Please, pour us each a glass of cognac and then join me here by the fire. We shall see if we can put matters to rights,' Holmes invited me considerately.

I lost little time in carrying out his suggestion and, after a sip or two of cognac and once our pipes were both fully under way, I detailed the experience of my trip to Clerkenwell in a manner that was as clinical and undemonstrative as I could manage.

In view of the cold, logical cynicism that Holmes had displayed earlier, I was very much surprised at the degree of attention that he was now affording the most singular narrative that I was laying before him. He allowed his pipe to burn itself out and closed his eyes tightly while he concentrated on my every word.

Without making a single comment, Holmes refilled his pipe, from the Persian slipper and moved slowly over toward the window.

'Evidently you have endured a most traumatic experience, Watson,' he began. I was most surprised that there was not a trace of sarcasm in his voice. He accepted my statement pragmatically and turned towards me with a look of genuine concern upon his face.

'These are, indeed, very dark waters that we are descending into,' he announced. 'Although I accept the authenticity of your every word, and I appreciate your interpretation of each experience, you must also understand that, to a man of science, the likelihood of a logical explanation must undoubtedly exist. What do you know of this London Spiritualist Temple of which Joseph Carlisle is such a hard-working and prominent member?'

'I am afraid that I know very little. Apart from the fact that the Fox sisters of Boston, who are respected and quite eminent in the field of spiritualism, strongly recommended Carlisle to Mrs Forrester when they last met. The temple itself has become as fashionable as the entire movement, yet it always appears to be in dire need of funding.'

Holmes did not respond to my reply. It was almost as if he was already in possession of that information and that he had been hoping to hear something new.

'Did you happen to discover for how long the housemaid, Nancy, has been in the employ of Mrs Forrester?' Holmes asked, to my surprise.

'I did not think that it was either relevant or important that I should do so,' I replied defensively. I glanced across at my friend and considered his features which were furrowed deep in concentration.

'Holmes, despite the apathy that you seemed to display when I broached the subject to you earlier, you are undoubtedly showing a greater interest in the matter than I would have given you credit for. Furthermore, I cannot, for the life of me, understand the relevance of the longevity of the maid's service.'

'Very likely not; yet my own enquiries have proved it to be of the utmost importance.'

'I had not realized that you had conducted your own enquiries. I understood that you were so deeply immersed in your own case that you were indifferent towards the plight of Mrs Forrester.'

'Oh, Watson, once again your assumptions have led you towards an erroneous conclusion. How could you have suspected your old friend of being indifferent towards a case as intriguing as this one surely is? Besides, the case that has preoccupied me for so long reached an earlier conclusion than even I would have anticipated.

'My own enquiries have revealed a great deal, although the source of that information is one of which you will undoubtedly disapprove. I refer to none other than Mr Langdale Pike!'

'It is not for me to either approve or disapprove of your associates and fonts of knowledge. Nevertheless, it is true to say that I consider Pike's column to be an example of the lowest form of gutter press imaginable. Therefore, I do find it difficult to reconcile the fact that you occasionally contribute to his literary bile.' I had not intended to conclude with such a dramatic admonishment of my friend, and I awaited his reaction to it with more than just a little apprehension. Mercifully, as it transpired, I need not have concerned myself.

'Bravo, old fellow, well said indeed!' Holmes appeared to be unusually amused by my rebuke and applauded my frankness with a clap of his hands.

'Under normal circumstances, naturally enough, I would agree with you. However, you must also consider the cause that we are both fighting for, namely the peace of mind of Mrs Cecil Forrester. Let me put this to you, if you will allow: if I just happened to be a fellow man of medicine and I had managed to create, within my laboratory, a life-threatening bacteria, how would you view me?'

'I would, undoubtedly, regard you as a dangerous and foolhardy chemist and a poor scientist!' I replied, without a moment's hesitation.

'That is exactly the kind of reaction that I would expect to receive from an honourable man of medicine such as you. However, if, as a result of my dubious experiment, I was also able to create a cure that would eventually save the life of millions, I wonder if you would then still view me as such a renegade?'

'Well of course I would not, but those two are hardly comparable scenarios!' I exclaimed. Then I detected a ripple of amusement moving around my friend's lips and I realized that he, too, thought his comparison was a little wide of the mark.

'Two disparate branches of science, I grant you, Watson, but the ultimate goal of both is the general good of all. I must confess, however, that his extravagant use of pomade is simply unforgivable!'

I could not help but share my friend's amusement at his trivial observation. However, once our pipes were alight once more, I asked Holmes to outline the information that he had gleaned from the designing columnist, Langdale Pike.

'The circles within which Pike moves professionally are quite familiar with the machinations of the spiritualist movement and their temple. I would not, for a single instant, make the claim that the motives of every one of its members are dubious. I am in little doubt that many of the movement's practitioners are genuine and sincere. Perhaps some of them actually believe that they are making contact with the spirit world, although you are already aware of my own views upon the existence of such a realm.

'Nevertheless, those who do believe in the reality of such a place do have their pain eased by a truly authentic medium. Sadly, for the purposes of your long-suffering friend, Joseph Carlisle is not one of those. Since Mrs Forrester's stay in New England, even the reputation of the Fox sisters has come under a cloud and, as a consequence, any recommendation cannot be taken at face value.'

Once Holmes had concluded his dissection of Carlisle and the entire movement of which he was an integral part, I found that I could contain myself no longer.

'So, Holmes, it would seem that, from the very outset, you have doubted my every word,' I said, feeling somewhat aggrieved at my friend's continued scepticism.

'No, that is not the case at all, my dear fellow. I am in little doubt that what you have reported to me of your experiences in Clerkenwell has been accurate in every detail. However, it is your interpretation of all that you have witnessed that is open to question.

'According to the dubious Langdale Pike, your friend, Joseph Carlisle, possesses every trick in the book and he does not balk at using them when given the opportunity to do so.' Holmes explained his point of view to me, with a quiet and patient tolerance. However, my reaction was by no means so tranquil.

'But, Holmes, I actually heard the glass move upon the table with my own ears! Equally, I definitely saw Carlisle's hands firmly clasped about those of the two women!' I protested, with more than just a little exasperation in my voice.

'No doubt, no doubt, but have you not also admitted that Carlisle contrived to successfully create an environment that was conducive to belief? As I have pointed out to you, on more than one occasion, our baser senses can be imperfect and therefore are not always to be trusted. Perhaps if you place more faith in your inner feelings and instincts, you might well begin to view your experience in Clerkenwell in an entirely different light. Do not allow your desire to help an old friend, as commendable as this quest surely is, to cloud your judgement.'

By now Holmes had abandoned his pipe for a cigarette and, as I lit one of my own, we both fell into a contemplative silence. I digested each one of his well-intentioned words and I soon found myself re-evaluating everything that I had seen and heard.

'What you have suggested is all very well,' I began, grudgingly, 'however, I am certain that Mrs Forrester will not be so easily dissuaded.'

'Perhaps you are correct, yet it is gratifying to note that the clouds that were once obscuring your sense of reason, are slowly beginning to disperse. There is no doubt that the light of logic, no matter how dim, is shining once again.'

Holmes seemed to take a certain mischievous pleasure from his disparaging compliment, and I could not conceal a smile of my own once I observed this.

'Your concern for the welfare of an old friend does you great credit, Watson, and we must now put matters to rights. Despite any misgivings that you might now have, it is absolutely essential that you attend the next gathering that has been arranged for the evening after next!' Holmes turned towards me with an intensity that had been absent earlier.

'I had anticipated from your use of the word 'we', that you would be accompanying me there on this occasion.' I felt certain that this was to have been Holmes's intention, especially as the other mysterious affair had already reached its satisfactory conclusion.

'Be assured, Watson, that I shall be there at the appointed time. Nevertheless, it is absolutely vital that you arrive in Clerkenwell alone, armed with whichever excuse for my absence that you deem to be appropriate,' Holmes replied obliquely.

'I dare say that I will be able to produce something suitable. However, I would much rather have a clearer understanding of your reasons for wishing to travel there alone,' I complained.

'Let us just say that if events unfold in the manner that I anticipate, it would be advantageous if my presence there remains undetected.' Holmes's reply was as infuriatingly enigmatic as I had feared that it would be.

'Surely that will be almost impossible if you arrive after the séance has already begun,' I persisted.

Holmes reacted to my erroneous assumption by shaking his head and smiling condescendingly.

'Watson, I plan to arrive there long before either Joseph Carlisle or your good self, but enough of all of your pointless questioning!' With that he turned his attention towards his violin and a moment later the lyrical tones of Bruch were wafting serenely around our rooms.

It was now obvious to me that Holmes had no intention of continuing our analysis, at least for the time being. So, I decided to retire for the night, prematurely, in the hope that some rest might ease the dull ache within my head. For all the good that was to do me, I might have saved myself the trouble.

Just before retiring, I sat by my bedroom window trying to rationalize my conversation with Holmes while smoking my final pipe of the day. This proved to be a serious error on my part as this endless mental debate resulted in nothing more than a frustrating and totally restless night. By 4.00 in the morning, I had given it up and abandoned my dishevelled bed, consoling myself with a small glass of port and a cigarette.

Exhaustion obviously won and I awoke with a jolt, still sitting near the open window. I felt heavy-eyed and had a painfully stiff neck. I went downstairs and was not surprised to discover that Holmes had not yet appeared for breakfast, as he was disposed towards keeping the most Bohemian of hours at times.

I washed and dressed, greeted Mrs Hudson, and ate a hurried meal. As there was still no sign of my friend I was resolved to spend a fruitful day at my surgery. I folded up the morning paper when a small headline suddenly caught my eye.

EXPLORER'S SON LOST AT SEA!

I read further to discover, to my astonishment, that this referred to none other than the fugitive Michael Landsbury. The ship on which he had secured a berth had gone down whilst approaching the Bay of Bengal, '*with all hands tragically lost*'.

I wondered if this was fate, or perhaps Divine retribution, but then I decided that there was no jewel, least of all a fake one, that was worth the loss of human life. I was convinced that the article would prove to be of more than just a passing interest to Holmes; therefore I folded over the paper appropriately and propped it up against the ashtray on the dining-table. I reasoned that there was more chance of him using that than there was of him using his breakfast plate!

I arrived at my surgery to discover a waiting-room that was surprisingly full. I had certainly not read anywhere of an ongoing epidemic, but I rolled up my sleeves and decided to throw myself into my work with both dedication and enthusiasm. As a consequence, by the time I had closed my surgery door behind the last of my grateful patients, I had reached a state of complete exhaustion. Furthermore, I realized, with some surprise, that throughout the entire day, not a single thought of Mrs Forrester and her quest for the spirit of Evangeline had entered my head. When I arrived back at 221b I did not even enquire as to Holmes's whereabouts and I waved aside Mrs Hudson's offer of a light supper, with a disgruntled growl.

Upon reaching my room, I pulled angrily at my collar before throwing myself down onto my bed, where I enjoyed the most restful night's sleep that I had had in ages. This was in spite of the certain knowledge that within a few short hours I would be confronting Joseph Carlisle once again.

By the time that I was prepared to leave for Clerkenwell, I realized with some disappointment that there had still been no word from Holmes. I was resigned to travelling there alone and had decided to arrive well ahead of the studious medium. Then, as I turned towards the door, I saw a small slip of paper that had been propped up against a cushion upon my favourite chair. It was a brief and simple note from Sherlock Holmes and it read as follows:

Watson, do not, under any circumstances, fail to take all necessary precautions. S H

The meaning of this was clear, for it was a phrase that Holmes had employed many times in the past. He clearly thought that it would be advisable to take my old army revolver with me to Clerkenwell, although the reason for this was not apparent to me. Despite his odious demeanour, I could not foresee any obvious threat from Joseph Carlisle.

Nevertheless, I followed Holmes's instructions with immediate obedience and even ensured that each barrel was loaded before I closed the chamber. As I slid the gun into my coat pocket, I could not even begin to wonder at the reasons behind Holmes's stark and ominous warning. At once a shudder of excitement ran through me at the very thought of it.

I stepped down from my cab outside the house of Mrs Forrester, a full hour before the appointed time. This gave me the opportunity to assure her that it was still not too late for her to cancel the evening, even at this hour, should she wish to. It also gave me the time to pour out a glass of port to steady my frayed nerves.

Even as those words of gentle persuasion left my lips, I could sense that they were falling upon stony ground.

'Oh, John, I appreciate your concerns, I really do,' Mrs Forrester responded. 'However, if there is still a chance, even one as remote as you profess it to be, that I might yet be able to say goodbye to my dear Evangeline, then I feel that I have to take it.'

'In that case I shall remain with you and support you in any way that I am able to.' Mrs Forrester smiled warmly and she squeezed my hand in appreciation of my declaration.

Then it suddenly occurred to me that it had been Mrs Forrester who had met me at the door and she had shown me through to the drawing-room herself.

'I do not see the maid, Nancy. Is she no longer with you?' I asked in some surprise.

'I am afraid that her mother has been taken rather poorly. I have allowed her to take the night off so that she might tend to her. Nancy has only been with me for a short while, only a few weeks in fact, yet during that time she has made herself indispensable,' she assured me.

'Was it not an unusual evening for you to grant her time off, as you were expecting a visit from Joseph Carlisle and myself?' I asked.

'John, I am not yet so frail that I am incapable of entertaining two gentlemen for a single evening!' she scolded me, but with a touch of humour in her tone.

'I am more than certain that you are.

However, is there not a chance that her absence might break Carlisle's circle around the table?'

'Carlisle has assured me that we shall not be joining hands around the table on this occasion. It will be an altogether different type of evening, the culmination of all that we have, so far, sought to achieve. You look astonished at hearing those words from me, but I assure you, John, that I am merely quoting from Carlisle.'

For what seemed an eternity, Mrs Forrester and I sat together in an atmosphere of silent expectation while we awaited the arrival of her guest.

From the very moment that Carlisle entered the room, I felt that each one of my natural defences had automatically become engaged. This was in spite of Carlisle's soft calming tones and the openness of his smile. Perhaps the impression of how he had been skirting around Mrs Forrester's bureau while she had been writing out his cheque, had stayed with me. The very thought of his greedy little fingers twitching feverishly while he had waited for her signature, filled me with the utmost repugnance.

Whatever was at the root of my feelings, I was now certain that I would have been in a far calmer state of mind had Holmes decided to travel down with me. Where was Holmes and why did he not come?

Of course, as Holmes had reminded me on those many occasions when his behaviour appeared to have been unfathomable to those of us who are mere mortals, his every word and action had a logical reason behind it. This thought certainly consoled me as I realized that Carlisle was poised to begin his ritual.

'Well, Dr Watson, I am certainly glad to see that you have decided to join us once again. Perhaps by the end of the evening you will have something positive to report back to Mr Holmes,' Carlisle suggested. 'It is a pity that he could not also be here. I suppose that there are affairs of state that have detained him once again.'

There was something that was almost contemptibly dismissive in Carlisle's tone when he uttered that last sentence.

'You may retain doubts as to his desire to be here, Mr Carlisle, but I can assure you that Mr Holmes has an almost insatiable appetite for knowledge. If it were at all possible for him to do so, there is no doubt that he would have attended your little demonstration here this evening!' I responded immediately.

'Well, it is certainly a shame, however, his absence will do nothing to detract from that which we hope to accomplish here on this auspicious night. We came so very close to a visualization of the spirit of Evangeline just two nights past, that I have very little doubt that some of your pain will be alleviated before we are finished, Mrs Forrester.'

Having made this earnest promise, Carlisle clasped her hands and guided her gently towards the doors that opened out on to the extensive gardens that were at the rear of the house.

'Now, Dr Watson, I trust that you will not object to assisting me in moving these chairs over towards the doors. We shall not be sitting within a circle on this occasion, as we shall all be facing out towards the lawn.'

Carlisle indicated the small, winged arm-chairs that were sitting on the far side of the room and we arranged them next to the one already occupied by Mrs Forrester without any difficulty. Carlisle then threw open the door with ceremonious effect, before taking his own position on the chair that was situated in the middle.

'I cannot but wonder at your reasons for deciding to alter your arrangements. After all, when we were sitting around the table, barely forty-eight hours ago, you maintained that we had come very close to success, there and then,' I could not help saying.

'All will become clearer to you before the

evening is over, Dr Watson, I can assure you,' Carlisle replied, somewhat inadequately.

He was on the point of reaching for our hands, when I excused myself on the grounds that I wished to smoke a quick pipe outside in the fragrant night air. Carlisle seemed to be somewhat put out by what he saw as an unnecessary delay and he implored me to be as brief as possible.

As I stepped out into the large and well maintained garden, I was immediately struck by a surreal and all pervading silence that belied the clear sky and the time of evening. There was no chorus of birds, nor even a light rustling of leaves, as one might have expected. As a matter of fact, the silence was so complete, that the sound I made on striking my match, appeared to echo around the entire garden.

Surely, I decided, if such a thing even existed, this would be a night when the spirits would certainly be abroad! The moon was full and high and its diaphanous glow cast every leaf and each blade of grass in a strange and spectral shadow. In spite of the balmy temperature, and against my better judgement, I then found myself shivering uncontrollably. Somehow I became convinced that on this night we were on the point of experiencing an event of some significance. However, the nature of what this would be, I could only speculate upon.

By this time I realized that I was, in all probability, creating as much anxiety for Mrs Forrester as I was for that erstwhile clairvoyant. Therefore, I decided to knock out my pipe against the side of an ornate, Renaissance-style flower urn and, with more than a slight feeling of unease, I finally took my allocated seat by the door.

I almost recoiled when Carlisle went to take me by the hand. However, I was determined to see this thing through. I have to admit that I was doing this as much for the sake of my own curiosity as it was for the good of Mrs Forrester, and finally I yielded. I was also thoroughly convinced that, at this advanced hour, Holmes had absolutely no intention of becoming involved in the night's proceedings.

I could not help but notice how closely Carlisle was studying my every movement. Had my behaviour aroused his curiosity? Could I also detect an anxiety that had not been present there before? Surely he had not realized that I was trying to give Holmes as much time as I could so that he might yet make a belated appearance.

Then I began to wonder at the reason behind Carlisle's agitation over the time.

After all, I had only been outside in the garden for a few minutes and yet he glanced repeatedly at his pocket watch, from the moment that I returned.

It was still quite early in the evening and surely the spirits were not restricted to a timetable! Perhaps Carlisle had already arranged another appointment elsewhere, later on that night,? Or perhaps there was another reason . . .

Suddenly, and with not a little force, Carlisle grabbed me by the hand. Almost at once he began to go into a trance similar to the one that we had witnessed two nights before. He threw his head back in that bizarre fashion and he squeezed his eyes tightly shut.

Once his eyes did reopen, I could see that his pupils had disappeared into the top of his eye sockets and his entire body began to shudder most violently! Beads of perspiration began to build profusely upon his contorted forehead and his complexion became deathly pale. Indeed, I had often held the hands of my patients as they lay upon their death-beds and they had contained more warmth in them than those of Joseph Carlisle at that moment.

I had no qualms keeping my wits about me and my eyes wide open, throughout the entirety of this most singular of rituals. This time there was to be no circle for me to break and, besides, Carlisle was now seated alongside of me and not directly opposite. If he were to keep his promise and tonight's evocation of the spirit of Evangeline were to prove to be a visual manifestation, then I was determined to ensure that I had a full understanding of everything that was supposed to have taken place.

In any event, by now he was surely totally oblivious to any or all of my thoughts and actions, for he now began to chant. Although I could not be certain, it seemed to me that the silent trance that Carlisle had remained in, prior to the chanting, was considerably shorter than it had been on the previous occasion. Nevertheless, he now began to call out to the spirit world.

'Oh spirits of our beloved dead, come to us now, for tonight you are truly exalted!'

He repeated this chant many times over and all the while the volume and the passion within his voice, gradually heightened. His grip upon my hand increased in its intensity and to such an extent that, once again, I found myself fearing for the well-being of Mrs Forrester.

I glanced across to her, but she appeared to be so spellbound by Carlisle's exhortations, that she was, to all appearances, oblivious to the discomfort of his grip. Indeed, I could not even be sure that she was similarly affected. She stared towards the garden, apparently convinced that, within a short while, she would see her beloved Evangeline once again.

'We know that you are many, yet there is only one of you that we seek this night . . . Evangeline!' Carlisle suddenly changed his chant and now repeated this new phrase again and again.

After a while he began to place a greater emphasis upon the name and eventually the remainder of the sentence was omitted from his dramatic plea for contact.

'Oh, Evangeline, please let us know if you are close to us. Your mother's love draws you ever nearer. Please show us that you are here!'

There appeared to be something close to desperation in Carlisle's voice now, as he continued to implore Mrs Forrester's daughter for a definite indication of her presence. Then it seemed as if Carlisle's efforts at breaking through were taking its toll upon his constitution, for he suddenly collapsed backward into his chair in a state of complete and absolute exhaustion.

His eyes closed once again and his breathing became unnaturally heavy and erratic. I was on the point of examining him, but before I had the opportunity to do so,

Mrs Forrester and I were alerted to an unexpected sound that seemed to be coming from the garden.

Under a set of different circumstances, it is doubtful that either of us would have scarcely noticed so innocuous a sound. However, such was the atmosphere that Carlisle had managed to create and so intense was the silence that existed outside, that even the light movement and sounds of a set of wind chimes now penetrated the night air with an awe-inspiring resonance.

The chimes were certainly faint and intermittent and yet they were unmistakable, nonetheless. I can assure you that never before had so gentle and harmonic a sound stirred within two people such a sense of wonderment and excitement.

Mrs Forrester and I glanced nervously towards each other and then, as if in answer to my questioning gaze, she stated emphatically, 'I can assure you, John, that I have never owned a set of wind chimes! Consequently, I have as little notion as to where that sound is coming from as you do.'

I acknowledged her assurance with a nod of my head and we both turned apprehensively towards Joseph Carlisle. Evidently, he had not been aware of the sound of the wind chimes, for his condition and his situation had not altered since we had heard the first sound.

However, I was just at the point of taking his pulse and examining him further when, with an alarmingly sharp exhalation of air, Carlisle suddenly sat bolt upright once more. His eyeballs almost shot out of their sockets and they were shining with a sightless gaze. At that very moment I could not be quite sure as to which was the more alarming prospect: the curious occurrence in the garden, or Carlisle's violent, physical reaction to his trance-like state. That question was about to be answered, but in a fashion that neither one of us could have possibly predicted or envisaged.

Gradually Carlisle's breathing began to return to normal and he appeared to be aware of his surroundings once more. So it was that the three of us first heard the singing at the same time.

That it was a female voice was beyond doubt, however, it was so light and distant that it was impossible to identify, even for Mrs Forrester. After a few minutes though, as the volume of the voice increased, I realized that the tune was somehow familiar to me. Nonetheless, I was not able to identify it before Mrs Forrester suddenly pulled me by the arm.

'Oh my goodness, John, that is surely Evangeline's favourite aria from the *Magic Flute*,' she exclaimed tearfully.

'You must calm yourself, Mrs Forrester. It is important that we keep a clear head. Although you might recognize the tune, can you be absolutely certain that the voice singing it is that of Evangeline?' I asked quietly.

'I cannot be sure, John, although you must know that she did not enjoy the sound of her own voice and, therefore, she would sing only rarely. However it was her favourite aria and that has to be more than a mere coincidence, surely.' She became overly excited once again, and at this moment I found myself at a loss for a single rational word.

'Was there anybody but yourself who knew of Evangeline's passion for this piece of music?' I asked, but before she could reply, we were both interrupted by the unpleasant sound of Carlisle's sarcastic laughter.

'Really, Dr Watson, you surprise me, you really do. I am aware that you are a man of science and that you are a prolific chronicler of your associate's championing of the cause of pure logic. I am certain, however, that even with a background such as yours, you must admit that tonight we are experiencing a series of events that defy all of the laws of logical thought.

'Tonight we are on the cusp of transcending the world of the living and that of the recently departed who now yearn for their final resting place. Open your heart and your mind, Dr Watson, I implore you!'

Mrs Forrester was clearly greatly impressed by Carlisle's impassioned plea.

'She must be here with us, John, for I am certain that there was nobody else who knew of her love for that aria. Oh, when might we finally be allowed to actually see her, Mr Carlisle?' she asked in a voice that was positively quivering with her fervour and expectation.

I, on the other hand, had not been so affected by Carlisle's portentous pronouncement, and to hear that Mrs Forrester had been reduced to such a condition was more than I could bear.

'Mr Carlisle,' I began sternly, 'you have promised much, and yet, so far, all that you have delivered is the sound of a glass moving upon a table, the jingle from a set of wind chimes and — '

It was at that precise moment, that the three of us first saw it! We were all attracted to it simultaneously and it left each of us both aghast and thrilled at the same time. There, at the furthermost end of the garden, could clearly be seen a faint, yet distinct, glimmer of a white and translucent light. Indeed, the light was so pale that, were it not for the fact that it was partly sheltered by dense, overhanging branches from apple trees that formed a small orchard, it would surely have been obliterated by the brightness of the full moon.

The light continuously rose and fell, behaving as if it were a pure white flame. Even from this distance it seemed to be moving from left to right and then back again, appearing as if it were trying to attract our attention. In this endeavour it was surely proving to be most successful.

Mrs Forrester let out a shrill cry of great excitement, in spite of the fact that the light had yet to assume any shape or form. I found myself becoming thrilled at the prospect of beholding an aspect of the unknown. Even Carlisle appeared to be incapable of any kind of spontaneous reaction. He remained silent and motionless, his mouth hanging open in wonder at the sight.

I found that it was impossible for me to sit still for a moment longer and I was determined to examine this apparition at closer quarters. I confirmed the presence of my revolver within my pocket and, as I lit a cigarette, I rose from my chair.

To my great surprise, and displaying a

reaction and force that defied his size and build, Carlisle forced me back down into my chair with the palm of his left hand.

'No, Dr Watson, you really must not!' he cried out desperately. 'This one impulsive action that you are proposing, will immediately undo all of the remarkable progress that we have so far made.' He continued to hold me down while he offered me this explanation.

I would surely have continued to struggle against this constriction, were it not for Mrs Forrester pleading with me to co-operate with Carlisle for a while longer.

'Oh please, John, just a little more patience, I beseech you! I am certain that Mr Carlisle is correct in what he says and, besides, we are so close to being with my beloved Evangeline once again.'

It was impossible for me to ignore so impassioned a plea from Mrs Forrester and although I removed Carlisle's hand, disdainfully, from my chest, I decided to remain in my chair and smoke my cigarette within the house after all.

'You must try to calm your nerves, Dr Watson, you really must, you know. After all, I can assure you that the spirits have no unfavourable intentions towards us.' I found that it was impossible to tell whether Carlisle intended to offer me genuine advice, or if he was merely patronizing me.

'You used the phrase 'these spirits', just then. Surely you are not implying that there is more than one here tonight?' I asked.

'Oh indeed. I can sense that we are surrounded by a good many at this very moment. Remember that, although we are only seeking the one, these wanderers of the spirit world are not nearly so selective.' There was such conviction in Carlisle's voice just then, that I decided to focus my attention more upon the inconceivable activity at the bottom of the garden, than upon the persistent doubts that continued to reverberate around my head.

We continued to gaze intently at the constantly evolving white light as it shimmered its way back and forth in the distance.

But then, wait . . . I could not believe what I was seeing and I felt a chill run down my spine. Had my eyes or my good sense started to deceive me? I could just make out the light beginning to assume a more definite shape. What manner of transformation was this spectral apparition now beginning to undergo?

There was, evidently, no doubt within the mind of Mrs Forrester that the light was assuming the outline of a female form. There was, equally, little doubt as to the identity of this spectral woman, for Mrs Forrester began to repeat the name of her daughter over and over again. She turned towards Joseph Carlisle for some words of comfort and of guidance. Carlisle did not fail her.

'Oh, Evangeline, come closer, my child. Please approach us and without fear. We mean you no harm, least of all from your devoted mother,' Carlisle chanted passionately.

By now there was little doubt that the shape of a woman was, indeed, being gradually defined by the light, although it gave us no sign that it had any intention of drawing closer to the house. This fact was clearly beginning to cause Mrs Forrester some agitation, for she now implored Carlisle to increase the intensity of his chanting.

'If it is Evangeline out there, why will she not come closer to me? Surely she must realize that she has nothing to fear from me,' she implored.

I thought that I would certainly go quite mad! Carlisle persisted with his incessant chanting while Mrs Forrester repeatedly summoned her daughter to approach us.

Then, at the moment when I was certain that events could not possibly take a more bizarre turn, Carlisle suddenly leapt up from his chair and began to flail his arms wildly above his head, as if signalling to the woman who was bathed in light. Strangely, his actions were beginning to assume the impression of a warning rather than the gesture of welcome that we had been anticipating and for which Mrs Forrester had beseeched him.

Almost immediately, the female spirit began to move hesitantly and uncertainly towards us. However, even at this closer proximity, we could still not make out her identity and her features remained very indistinct.

Somewhat breathlessly, Mrs Forrester now confirmed that the size and build of the apparition corresponded to those of her daughter. However, her true identity contin-ued to be clouded by the flickering glow that constantly surrounded her.

I could not, for the life of me, understand by what means Carlisle had suddenly become able to exert so much control over an entity as capricious as the glowing phantom had been up to now. As Carlisle stopped waving his arms, so the spirit seemed to stop in her tracks. As a matter of fact, she almost appeared to take a step or two away from us once more.

I should point out that when I say that she took a step, her actual movement could be described as gliding, or almost floating above the lawn. As if he was able to sense my next question, Carlisle suddenly explained.

'You must try to understand, Doctor, that

at present our contact with Evangeline is still only a most fragile one. At any moment that connection could be broken and then she might be lost to us, perhaps for all time!'

Despite her most understandable anxiety and impatience, Mrs Forrester considered Carlisle's last statement and decided to await Evangeline's next approach with as much quiet calm as she could. I lit another cigarette and reluctantly anticipated the next development. When this did occur it turned out to be as dramatic as it was unexpected. Without a minute's warning, Carlisle suddenly got up from his chair and ran over to grab his satchel which he had left by the table in the centre of the room. Mrs Forrester and I were both aghast and confused at this strange behaviour. However, once we turned our attention back to the events in the garden, we saw a possible cause for the sudden change in Carlisle's conduct.

Immediately I pulled out my gun and advised Carlisle to sit back down while events continued to unfold before us. I took this drastic action because I was left in no doubt that Carlisle was poised to beat a frantic and hasty retreat.

'Mr Carlisle!' Mrs Forrester exclaimed. 'What is the meaning of this?'

Mr Carlisle's complexion became paler

than it had been when he was in his supposed trance. With resignation and dejection he placed his bag back down on the floor and shuffled back to his chair.

The reason for the bizarre nature of Carlisle's transformation soon became clear to us: the movements of the female apparition had suddenly become frantic and disorientated. No longer was she gliding serenely back and forth. She seemed to be struggling to make her way to the far end of the garden and further away from the house.

Mrs Forrester called after her repeatedly; however, it was obvious, even to her, that there was very little chance of her daughter's ghost making an appearance. With an air of heartbreaking resignation, she merely sat there, still and pale. Carlisle continued to stare down the barrel of my gun.

Then we heard voices calling to each other from the far end of the garden. One of these, naturally enough, was a female voice, although one look at the face of Mrs Forrester was all I needed to know that it was not the voice of her beloved daughter. Yet, it sounded vaguely familiar, even from that distance.

'Oh, Nancy ... how could you?' Mrs Forrester shook her head slowly, as recognition dawned upon her. 'She gained my confidence, I trusted her completely. When she was brushing my hair, I would talk to her of Evangeline. I just sat there, talking, talking . . . '

'Nancy, the maid, but why would she be out there?' I asked.

Mrs Forrester suddenly jumped up from her chair with a rage and energy of which I would not have thought her capable, and began lashing out at Carlisle's face. With my gun still firmly on him, Carlisle offered no resistance to this onslaught and soon his face was a mass of red welts and cuts from Mrs Forrester's long, elegant nails.

'You evil, malicious man!' Mrs Forrester screamed over and over again, until once she was utterly spent, she collapsed back into her chair, sobbing uncontrollably.

Using the barrel of my gun, I directed Carlisle to walk ahead of me and out into the garden. I certainly had no intention of allowing my eyes to leave this rogue for even a single instant. As I stood there, watching and listening, I realized that at least one of the other voices was familiar to me. Furthermore, as the female shape continued her slow approach towards the house, I became aware of other shapes that were following carefully behind her, although they were still, temporarily, obscured by the fading light. As they drew ever closer, I soon recognized one of those forms very well indeed!

'Holmes, is that really you?' I called, in a tone that said as much about my state of confusion as it did of my sense of relief.

'Well done, Watson!' Holmes called back, as he was, evidently, pleased to note that I had already apprehended the scurrilous Joseph Carlisle.

By now they were almost upon us and I was undecided as to which of the four people approaching, I was the more surprised to see. As to their reasons for being there, well, that was becoming clearer to me with each passing minute.

Apart from Holmes and Nancy, the maid, there was also our old friend from Scotland Yard, Inspector Lestrade and another gentleman of dubious appearance, whom I recognized from Holmes's earlier description of him. The pomade, the luxuriant hair and the ivory cigarette holder, told me that Mr Langdale Pike had also become involved in the premature conclusion of the maid's charade. Pike immediately pointed an accusing finger towards Joseph Carlisle.

'Yes, Inspector, that is certainly the man in question.' Pike ran forward and almost took out one of Carlisle's eyes with his garish cigarette holder, so enthused was he at being able to single him out.

Once they were all in the room, and before any explanations were offered, I was much relieved when Lestrade responded to Pike's identification of Carlisle by clapping that sorry individual into a set of handcuffs. At last I could relax my gun arm, which had now been extended for some considerable time.

I was more than a little surprised to note that the wrists of Nancy were similarly endowed to those of Carlisle, and Holmes led her forcibly towards the chair next to that of the bogus clairvoyant. She struggled, in vain, and astonished us all with her vile range of expletives.

Holmes made certain that she was secure and, having noted our surprise at his treatment of her, he dramatically announced, 'Please allow me to introduce you all to Mrs Joseph Carlisle!'

'Nancy, are you really married to this awful creature?' Mrs Forrester asked in some dismay. 'Why would you betray me in such a way?'

'For the money, pure and simple,' the woman snapped back sharply. She made no attempt to avoid the look of pain which was etched all over the face of her former employer. Indeed, she stared directly back at Mrs Forrester with a glare of such spiteful defiance that my old friend was clearly shaken to the core.

'Oh yes, and if it had not been for this gentleman over here and his interfering ways, we should have got a good deal more out of you, for sure!' She glared and pointed angrily towards me while she continued with her vitriolic outburst.

'Nancy, how could you do this to me? My goodness, we spent so many hours together talking to each other that it seems almost inconceivable to me,' Mrs Forrester lamented despairingly.

'Those talks, they seemed like they would go on forever. By the way, my name is actually Annie, not that it matters now, of course.

'I told you that we should have stopped after that last session, you damned fool!' Annie had now turned her attention and her viper's tongue towards her husband, who merely raised his eyes to the heavens despondently.

Surprisingly, Annie spoke with a very strong cockney accent that belied the modulated tones of her husband. Still, crime does seem to bring together the most diverse of bedfellows. Naturally enough, especially as I was in the presence of Mrs Forrester, the example of Jonathan Small and his most singular companion, Tonga, immediately sprang to mind.

At that moment I noticed that Langdale Pike had suffered some sort of injury and that there was blood seeping through the left sleeve of his garish, light-grey suit jacket. There was also a jagged tear in the shoulder of that most singular of garments, which told me of a knife wound. As if to confirm my diagnosis, with a sardonic smile Pike held up a large switch blade so that all could see the cause of his wound.

'As you can see, this she-devil also comes armed and with a blade that is every inch as sharp as her tongue,' Pike declared, while he waved the arm in question, in a most cavalier fashion.

He was certainly making light of his injury, but I could see that he was growing quite pale and that the patch of crimson was expanding in a most alarming way. My Hippocratic oath would not allow me to leave Pike unattended, although, in truth, I had never before applied my medical knowledge to a less deserving soul. Mrs Forrester directed me to the towels and some hot water and, before long, I had Pike's wound tightly strapped up and his arm secured in a makeshift sling.

'I do thank you, Dr Watson, although I sense that you don't altogether approve of me.' Pike smiled, while displaying a single gold tooth.

'I do not think that I have known you long or well enough, sir, for me to be able to form that sort of judgement. However, if you were to ask me if I approve of your profession, then I would have had to say that I do not!' I responded earnestly.

Pike bowed, no doubt in acknowledgement of my honesty, before Holmes decided to intervene on his behalf.

'Do not be too hasty in your judgement, Watson. After all, Pike's assistance has ensured that your friend, Mrs Forrester, will not have to endure any more pain and anxiety than she has done already.'

It was only now that he had finally spoken, that I realized just how silent Holmes had actually been from the moment that he entered the room. He had been standing by the windows while he smoked, no doubt waiting for the initial commotion to die down. Suddenly he turned towards me, wearing a most challenging smile.

'Ah, Watson, I can hear the sound of a thousand questions rushing to cascade from the tip of your tongue. Now that you have completed your most excellent ministrations, perhaps I can finally clarify certain things for you?'

'I could do with some clarification myself,' Inspector Lestrade complained, while he brought out his notebook and pencil. 'I am not always at your beck and call, you know, Mr Holmes. Chasing down here to Clerkenwell on a whim, I must say. Ghosts and charlatans, indeed!'

'You must calm yourself, Inspector, for I can say without a doubt that you shall achieve far more here tonight, than ever you would do from behind your desk back at Scotland Yard!' Holmes tried to assure him with one of his winning smiles.

'Well, that remains to be seen. I suppose that your ideas and theories have been of some small use to us over the years,' Lestrade conceded grudgingly.

'Hah! Well, that is most gratifying to note. Then I suppose I can rely upon you to indulge me for this one further time?' Holmes suggested.

Lestrade responded to this by taking to a seat from where he could keep a close eye upon both of the Carlisles and he opened up his notebook with a steely intent.

At that moment I asked Holmes if he would indulge me with a quiet word outside, for I felt much aggrieved at his shabby treatment of me, once again! Holmes agreed without a moment's hesitation and he spun around on his heels while I offered my apologies for the delay to both Mrs Forrester and Inspector Lestrade, before I joined him outside.

We walked across the lawn until I was certain that we were out of the earshot of others. However, I was soon to discover that I was not to have my say, after all.

'You know, Watson, I owe you and Mrs Forrester a thousand apologies. I really had no idea just how affected that you both might have been by the theatrics of the infamous Mr and Mrs Carlisle. However, you must try to understand that I could not have intervened until the moment that things had reached such a pass that I could convince Lestrade of the Carlisles' criminal intent. After all, pretending to move a glass around upon a table is hardly the same as the impersonation of another,' Holmes explained.

'You might have confided in me, Holmes,' I responded, determined that I should not be put off on this occasion. 'I am sure that I can be relied upon to carry out your every instruction.'

'Of course you can, Watson, but can you tell me, in all honesty, that you would have reacted in the same way if you had possessed prior knowledge of my intent? Besides, I know, only too well, that you would not have allowed Mrs Forrester to endure her anguish, even for a second, if you were certain that the entire thing was nothing more than a charade.'

Holmes delivered this outrageous statement in such a clinical fashion that it was all that I could to do to contain my rage.

'You have used us, Holmes, and caused untold grief to a dear, old friend who has already suffered much. You must realize that the end does not always justify the means,' I suggested sternly.

The manner in which Holmes looked at me, after I had delivered this heartfelt rebuke, did not convince me that he understood the point that I was trying to make. I wondered if he was even capable of that kind of understanding. In his pursuit of justice he would, invariably, make any form of sacrifice that he thought necessary, even on behalf of others, in order to achieve his goal.

'Watson, the end, in this instant, is to ensure that those venomous vultures will never again be able to prey upon the weaknesses of the bereaved. Mrs Forrester has certainly not been their first victim, nor would she have been their last, save for our timely intervention.'

In the face of Holmes's undeniably logical response, it was impossible for me to raise any further argument. I suppose that I should not have expected to have received any other from a man who possessed a mind such as his. We walked slowly back to the house in an introspective silence that spoke volumes.

The delay that resulted from our brief conference certainly brought about a change in Carlisle's attitude. No longer did he appear to be as crestfallen and defeated as he had been previously, and he was fervently protesting against what he saw as his unfairly forced detention.

'What charges are to be brought against me that might justify my arrest? Surely it is not a crime to have failed to satisfy the needs of our client. After all, our access to the spirit world cannot simply be turned on and off like a tap!' These words of defiance from Carlisle were clearly being encouraged and provoked by his ever contentious wife.

'That does not seem to be an unreasonable request,' Lestrade commented, while turning, hopefully, towards Holmes for an answer.

'It is a question that is easier to answer than you might expect, Lestrade,' Holmes responded. 'This wretched couple are to be charged with nothing less than fraud and embezzlement and on a good many counts.'

'Do you have the proof with which to substantiate these claims?' the inspector asked. He had clearly observed the furtive glances that were exchanged by the Carlisles and consequently the tone of his question was less cynical than it had been previously.

'You may have observed me collecting a variety of objects from the garden which are now gathered here in this sack.'

I had not even noticed the small canvas bag that was sitting unobtrusively by the back door until it was brought to our attention. With a typical theatrical flourish, Holmes now emptied the contents onto the floor.

A strange selection of unusual items was strewn across the rug. There was a long, flowing white gown, fashioned from a fine shimmering silk; next to this lay two small lanterns, each of which had been shrouded in a piece of white gauze that would have altered the shade of its natural light. Predictably, the other item was a set of wind chimes.

'I do not think that I need to demonstrate the kind of effect that these items would have had upon any innocent and distant onlookers,' Holmes proclaimed, as he glared at each one of us in turn. Even Lestrade appeared to understand the significance of these props. I noticed the veil with which Annie Carlisle had concealed her face as she moved around the garden during her ghostly dance.

'I can guarantee that if we had arrived even

a short while later, these props, together with this would-be actress, would have disappeared as vaporously as had their failed illusion!' Holmes's raised voice echoed round the silent room.

I noticed that Carlisle's head dropped down still lower than it had been and even his wife looked blankly into the distance.

'As if further proof might still be needed,' Holmes continued, 'I am certain that a brief examination of that satchel over there will reveal a most realistic pair of theatrical fake hands. Of course, I do not need to explain that by placing those within the hands of the two women, Carlisle was then able to move the glass around the surface of the table, as he pleased, unhindered and without breaking the circle.' Holmes spread out his arms in front of him as if expecting applause from a captivated and beguiled audience, which we surely were. All of us, that is, save for the dogged and persistent Inspector Lestrade.

'Again, I must ask you, Mr Holmes, where is the crime? After all, the props that you have so proudly displayed, and the use for which they have been put, would, in all likelihood, be thrown out of a court of law as being nothing more serious than the tools of a harmless prank!' he exclaimed, and not without good reason.

However, in the face of this barrage of exchanges, we had all lost sight of the only tangible victim, the forlorn and now disillusioned Mrs Cecil Forrester. She seemed oblivious to everything that Holmes and Lestrade had just said and she just sat in a melancholy silence, while her vacant eyes did not move from the bottom of the garden, even once.

I pointed Lestrade in the direction of this sorry sight.

'I would say that it was not such a harmless prank, after all, eh, Lestrade?' I said, somewhat sombrely. The inspector reddened as he cleared his throat.

'Well . . . of course, that is a different matter altogether. Obviously if there is a way of bringing these scoundrels to book for the pain that they have so obviously caused, then I surely will.'

'Well said, Inspector!' Holmes applauded Lestrade with a single, resounding clap that also aroused Mrs Forrester from her despondent reverie.

'However, we must not forget the cheque that Watson here so surreptitiously observed Mrs Forrester hand over to Carlisle, two nights ago. I am certain that earlier cheques have been cashed by now, so there is your case for embezzlement and fraud, Lestrade,' Holmes pronounced and Mrs Forrester confirmed that some of the cheques had already cleared from her account.

'There is also the small matter of assault, which bears some consideration,' Langdale Pike reminded us, somewhat sheepishly, while holding his bandaged arm aloft for all to see.

'Not for the first time, Mr Holmes, you have presented me with my case and once again, I congratulate you,' Lestrade acknowledged generously.

Holmes waved this aside with the briefest of smiles and then suggested that Mrs Forrester should hand her chequebook over, into the inspector's care.

'I can assure you, Inspector Lestrade, that my name need not appear at all,' Holmes said, while at the same time indicating to Lestrade that the Carlisles should now be removed from the presence of the long-suffering Mrs Forrester. Now that the formalities had been all but concluded, he was certain that she need not tolerate them under her roof for a moment longer than she had to.

Lestrade immediately summoned his constables and a moment later that awful couple, together with their sack and satchel, were dragged unceremoniously from the room. Lestrade was on the point of joining them, but he was held back once he heard my next question, so he sent his men ahead of him, back to Scotland Yard.

'Holmes, you have explained everything, with your customary clarity and sound logical reasoning, save for one thing: you have yet to set out the chain of events that led you to be here tonight in the first place.'

'Yes, Mr Holmes, I should like to know the answer to that one myself. I could tell from John's manner that your international entanglements were just a ruse that allowed you to avoid the proceedings that you held in such disdain.' Mrs Forrester's voice and manner had almost returned to normal.

'You are quite correct, madam, when you state that I did not attach too much credence to Joseph Carlisle and his outlandish claims. However, that is not to say that genuine clairvoyants do not exist, or that in some instances their work might have a meritorious effect. Carlisle, though, has proved himself to be the worst kind of fraudster. This is not normally my province, as Watson will, no doubt, confirm. For the answer to your question, I must refer you to my professional acquaintance, Mr Langdale Pike!'

Holmes made this announcement with the bravado of a master of ceremonies, a manner that, under the circumstances, I found to be totally out of place. He then lit a cigarette and promptly turned his back upon the entire proceedings.

Pike seemed to take an absolute age before he responded to Holmes's rousing introduction. He slowly took his place upon one of the chairs that had just been vacated and crossed his legs for maximum effect, as if he had spent hours rehearsing the process. By the time that he had lit his cigarette and appeared ready to explain himself, Lestrade and I were as close to exasperation as one could imagine.

'Despite the harsh judgement that Dr Watson has levelled against my profession, you must understand that I do provide a service of sorts, other than the lining of my pockets, although I confess that in the case of the latter, I have proved to be satisfyingly successful. Be that as it may, Mr Holmes will tell you I spend most of my time luxuriating upon my favourite corner seat within the first floor lounge of my club in St James's.

'My situation there is well known to all who move within my limited circle and, as a consequence, I rarely have to stir myself in order to seek out the latest tittle tattle.' Pike paused only long enough to emit a column of noxious Turkish tobacco smoke and to display his gold tooth when he smiled at the pleasure that he so obviously derived from his cherished club.

'As you might imagine, therefore, Mr Holmes is by no means my only regular caller at the club. As he might have already mentioned to you, Dr Watson, our association is based upon a mutual exchange of information and his practice flourishes as surely as does my column, as a result of it. I might aid him in exposing a card cheat, or a forger of fine arts, while he might top up my column with a marital scandal involving an influential eastern potentate. In our own way, we are both performing a dubious service and it is one that invariably produces a beneficial rather than a detrimental outcome.

'Although I could not, in all honesty, describe Mr Holmes as one, my agency has often resulted in the forging of many close friendships. In those instances, believe it or not, Dr Watson, the notion of exposing or scandalizing the name of these friends has always been abhorrent to me. Not only because of the loss of trust that might come about from this, but also it would surely result in the damming up of one of the channels that now fill my reservoir of information.'

By now I was beginning to find Pike's extravagant and fatuous style of speech, tiresome in the extreme. However, I was spared the chore of having to chastise Pike on a second occasion, by the timely intervention of

300

an unexpected ally, Inspector Lestrade.

'With all due respect, sir,' he began impatiently, 'time is getting on and I have yet to write anything in my notebook!'

Behind me I could hear Holmes chuckling under his breath as he moved further out into the garden so that he could avoid any further examples of his acquaintance's verbosity.

'Well, I must say, Detective, you certainly are not one to bandy words. Very well then, the simple facts are these: I believe that I can safely count Lord Hector Landsbury as one of the closest friends that I have made at my club, so far.

'No doubt, Mr Holmes has already told you of the unfortunate incident concerning the theft of the Sapphire of Thebes?' Pike asked me.

'Indeed he has. It must have been an awful business for the whole family,' I blurted out, thoughtlessly. As I made this comment I could hear Holmes emit a snarl of disapproval at this betrayal of confidence and he immediately moved back into the room.

'Well, that is most unfortunate; however, I trust that I might rely upon your discretion and your assurance that this tale will not find its way into your excellent collection of cases until an appropriate time has elapsed.'

It was gratifying to note that Pike did at

least have some respect for his personal friends, and I confirmed that I would withhold this case indefinitely, whilst mouthing an apology to Holmes.

'Of more public knowledge is the fact that Lord Landsbury's son, Michael, was tragically lost at sea when his berth went down while crossing the Bay of Bengal,' Pike continued.

'It was most kind of you to have left that story for my attention, Watson. However, I must confess that I was already privy to the knowledge from another source.' Holmes gestured towards Pike while he spoke.

'I am sorry, gentlemen, but I fail to see the relevance of any of this sapphire business and the Bay of Bengal!' Understandably, Inspector Lestrade was becoming increasingly frustrated by Pike's meandering narrative and his weaselly features reddened whilst his lips tightened in frustration.

'I know something of the matter because of the jewel's disappearance together with that of the thief himself, but where is the connection?' Lestrade pleaded.

'Be patient, Lestrade, surely a few minutes either way will not concern you when we are so close to a conclusion,' Holmes mollified the agitated inspector quietly. He then encouraged Pike to continue, with a broad sweep of his arm, and the columnist immediately obliged.

'Inspector, I am certain that your knowledge of the Thebes sapphire affair does not extend to the fact that the jewel was stolen by none other than the aforementioned Michael Landsbury!'

Holmes prevented Lestrade from a further interruption by placing a restraining hand upon the detective's left shoulder.

'With the limited knowledge that you possess of this singular family drama, it might well be hard for you to understand that young Michael actually took the jewel as a means of preventing a potentially devastating family scandal. Furthermore, his mother announced Michael's tragic loss to the press for exactly the same reason. Yet, there was one consequence of this public announcement that the Landsburys could not have foreseen: this was namely the attention that it immediately aroused amongst the members of the London Spiritualists Temple. I have encountered their practitioners upon a number of occasions. Indeed, one or two of them can even be counted among the members of my club. I can state, with some certainty, that a good many of them are certainly gifted and are sincere in what they do. It must also be said that there are frauds and charlatans amongst their number. Of these, Joseph Carlisle has accrued the least enviable reputation and he is generally shunned by all who know him.

'Therefore, you can well understand my consternation upon discovering that this awful fellow had presented himself at the Landsburys' front door within hours of the announcement having been made. I was actually present in the house at the time of his visit, and so it fell to me to greet him in the drawing-room. The Landsburys had excused themselves on the pretext of their grief, and I actually had to feign some form of civility towards the creature.'

Pike was now warming to his task and he lit another cigarette as a means of quelling his growing excitement, as he was clearly approaching the conclusion of his story.

'I do not understand,' I began, whilst taking advantage of this brief, but welcome intermission. 'You have used the word 'pretext' in your description of the Landsburys' grief. Are we to suppose, therefore, that his ship did not go down on its way to India?' I asked.

'No, not at all, that part of the story is tragically most accurate. However, it is also true to say that, somewhat fortuitously, Michael Landsbury had actually secured a berth on board a clipper that was bound for the East, a full week earlier.

'As I had been partially responsible for the wider circulation of the news of Michael's supposed loss, you might well appreciate the difficulty that I had in suppressing my amused indignation, when the news of that fellow's arrival was announced to me. I can assure you all, that our brief interview surely tested my acting abilities to their limit! It was difficult enough for me to have to feign grief at the tragic loss of my close friend's son; having then to extend polite hospitality to one such as Carlisle was more than my poor nerves could take. The very effrontery of the man, as he sat there sipping the Landsburys' tea, while, with each cup, he was plotting to exploit their grief for his own financial gain, was new to my experience. Naturally, I could not express my rage. If I had done so, it would surely have betrayed the Landsburys' trust and led to consequences that might well have brought about the ruination of the whole family. However, I was duty bound to inform him, in no uncertain terms, that the Landsburys would not contemplate his activities under their own roof for a single instant. I should say that despite the force of my rebuttal, the damnable man would not be put off.' Pike paused to empty his holder into a nearby ashtray.

'The blackguard!' I exclaimed.

'I cannot believe that I was a fool enough to allow that devil incarnate under my own roof. What a gullible old lady I truly am.' Mrs Forrester was shaking with rage, together with profound regret.

'You must not chastise yourself, Mrs Forrester, for you must remember that Hades himself was a most persuasive individual.' Pike's attempt at consoling the poor woman was only partly successful. Pike then continued, while attempting to mimic the voice of Joseph Carlisle.

'*Oh, Mr Pike, you really must try to persuade the Landsburys, for I am certain that I can help to ease the pain of their tragic loss. Even during the brief time that I have been here, I have sensed the presence of their dead son's tortured spirit.* Carlisle made this entreaty with all of the sincerity that his dark soul could muster.

'*The spirit does not conform to any of our boundaries, you know, and I am certain that Michael would have dragged himself from the very bowels of the ocean in order for him to return, once more, to the home of his beloved family.*

'I could scarcely believe my ears! Even while we were engaged in our bizarre and unsavoury conversation, I know only too well that Michael was, in all probability, sipping a pink gin upon the veranda at his uncle's tea plantation safely in the Punjab!'

'Hah! Well there cannot be any clearer indication of Carlisle's criminal intent than that,' Holmes confirmed with some excitement. 'Thank you, Pike,' he continued. 'By coming here with us tonight, and by your identification of Joseph Carlisle, you surely will have provided Inspector Lestrade with all the ammunition that he will need to press ahead with a successful prosecution.

'However, should the need arise, and the Landsburys find it impossible to give evidence at the trial, I assure you that I shall use all of my energy and powers to ensure that the Carlisles are not allowed to ply their nefarious trade for many years to come.

'Mrs Forrester, I shall ensure that every penny which they have extorted from you will be repaid in full, even I if I have to raid the Carlisles' bank account myself!'

'Now steady on, Mr Holmes, you must not forget that I am a policeman, when all is said and done,' Lestrade reminded Holmes with a smile, while he got up from his chair.

'Well, thank you, Mr Pike. Your explanation has certainly cleared up a good many things and I am certain that I will now be able to proceed with confidence,' Lestrade said. He rubbed his hands together gleefully as he, doubtlessly, contemplated yet another feather in his cap.

He bowed towards Mrs Forrester and shook us all by the hand before he took his leave.

'I shall be requiring statements from each of you over the next few days,' Lestrade reminded us on his way to the door.

'Thank you, Lestrade, and good night,' Holmes called after his former adversary.

'I admit that his rather limited abilities and his total lack of imagination are partially compensated for by his resolute doggedness and a genuine desire to see justice done.' This was surely the closest thing to a compliment that I was ever likely to hear from Holmes in reference to the man from Scotland Yard.

'Well, I for one shall require at least three days of complete rest to aid my recovery from my exertions here tonight,' Pike remarked, as he raised himself with his one functioning hand. 'I sincerely hope, Dr Watson, that you will now hold me in a somewhat more positive light,' Pike asked of me as we shook hands.

'The service that you have rendered here certainly might enable me to view you and your column more favourably,' I conceded.

'Well then, that will have to do, I suppose. It is certainly reassuring to know that Sherlock Holmes is associated with such a champion of morals.' We were treated to one last glimpse of Pike's golden tooth and he flung his muffler flamboyantly around his neck, before he took his leave.

Despite the lateness of the hour and her obvious emotional exhaustion, Mrs Forrester insisted that Holmes and I remain long enough for a fortifying glass of port and one final pipe.

As I observed how sympathetic Holmes's manner towards Mrs Forrester had become, I found that the annoyance that I had felt earlier was slowly dissipating. Consequently, our return journey to Baker Street was undertaken in a more convivial atmosphere than I might otherwise have imagined.

In the aftermath of the traumas that we had both just experienced, somehow it was most reassuring to note that it was our old friend, Dave 'Gunner' King, who held the reins of our cab that night.

'Off on another one of our adventures, are we, gentlemen?' King called down cheerily and expectantly.

'No, not tonight, King. A slow and sedate journey back to Baker Street, if you please,' Holmes replied. In spite of this request, King still moved off at a fair old lick, until Holmes reminded him with a rap on the roof from his cane.

'You must not judge my apparent lack of

human empathy too harshly, Watson. When your mind is of such a bent as mine, the consumption of relevant facts and the pursuit of logical reasoning and observation can very often result in the preclusion of any form of sympathetic regard for the feelings of others. That is not to say, however, that they are entirely absent, merely that they are temporarily and subconsciously repressed.'

This unusually frank admission by Holmes caught me completely unawares and I was not immediately capable of offering any form of a coherent response. I slowly lit my pipe before I made my reply.

'Equally, perhaps I should train myself to become more detached in certain situations,' I suggested, although, in truth, my primary intention was to further cement our reconciliation.

Holmes suddenly turned on me, with a look of unusual and startling intensity.

'No, Watson, you must not change, I implore you! You provide me with a grounding that is absolutely necessary for someone in my line of work.'

'As you wish, Holmes,' I agreed quietly, and I noted a smile of contentment as Holmes lit up a pipe of his own.

We smoked in silence for the remainder of the journey, although this was a far more comfortable silence than the one that we had experienced a short while earlier in the garden of Mrs Forrester.

Mercifully, Mrs Hudson had prepared for us both a light, cold supper and I was surprised to note that Holmes devoured his with as much voracity as I did. We concluded our meal with a cognac and cigar by the fire.

'For somebody who has displayed a marked apathy towards the matter from the very outset, you have certainly managed to emerge from the affair in total triumph.' I raised my glass to Holmes, by way of a salute.

'I cannot, in all honesty, derive any professional satisfaction from its conclusion. After all, my faculties were hardly pushed to their limits. Nevertheless, it is certainly gratifying for me to note that a personal friend of yours will no longer have to endure the intrusion of Joseph Carlisle in her life. Perhaps we might all learn that sometimes certain matters should be left to follow their own natural course. For surely, there is nothing that is a more integral part of our existence than death itself,' Holmes concluded.

'Well, I for one would have to think long and hard before attending another ceremony of the like,' I affirmed, while I threw the remains of my cigar into the fire and I drained my glass.

'Good night, old fellow,' I called out on the way to my room.

Holmes smiled towards me, without uttering another word. Then, despite the lateness of the hour, I saw him reach over and take up his violin, with a look of contentment upon his face.

I had not forgotten my pledge and barely a fortnight passed that did not find me in Clerkenwell and taking tea with Mrs Forrester. This was a practice that I maintained right up to the moment that she sadly passed away, barely three months after the loss of her daughter, Evangeline.

I found it was impossible to diagnose the exact cause of her death, principally because the damage caused by a broken heart cannot be accurately gauged, but I sincerely hoped that the two of them would now be reunited once again.

On the day of the funeral, a few of Mrs Forrester's oldest and dearest friends gathered at the house for the last time to pay their respects and final farewells. Long after the others had departed, I found myself lingering at the bottom of the garden. I was lost amongst the haunting shadows that were cast by the full moon and within my own thoughts.

I had now reached the conclusion that if anything positive could be derived from the whole sorry Carlisle saga, it was my own realization that the spirit, or soul, remains behind, long after the body has departed. This thought gave me surprising comfort, as I stood there beneath Mrs Forrester's favourite trees.

Then I heard it . . . A sound that chilled me right through to my very core. The sound was light, but yet distinct. It was both unmistakable and inexplicable. The sound rose above the rustling of the branches and my own erratic breathing

It was the sound of a set of wind chimes . . .

We do hope that you have enjoyed reading this large print book.

Did you know that all of our titles are available for purchase?

We publish a wide range of high quality large print books including:
Romances, Mysteries, Classics
General Fiction
Non Fiction and Westerns

Special interest titles available in large print are:
The Little Oxford Dictionary
Music Book
Song Book
Hymn Book
Service Book

Also available from us courtesy of Oxford University Press:
Young Readers' Dictionary
(large print edition)
Young Readers' Thesaurus
(large print edition)

For further information or a free brochure, please contact us at:
Ulverscroft Large Print Books Ltd.,
The Green, Bradgate Road, Anstey,
Leicester, LE7 7FU, England.
Tel: (00 44) 0116 236 4325
Fax: (00 44) 0116 234 0205

Other titles published by
The House of Ulverscroft:

SHERLOCK HOLMES AND THE GIANT RAT OF SUMATRA

Paul D. Gilbert

In the autumn of 1898, the people living and working in London's Docklands are astonished by the arrival of a long overdue clipper, the *Matilda Briggs*, which has apparently drifted into a vacant berth. On board, the only member of the crew remaining is a young cabin boy — and he is close to death, following a mysterious attack. The great consulting detective Sherlock Holmes is called to investigate the matter, but what will he uncover? A violent confrontation on the waterfront brings this story to a shocking conclusion . . .

THE DOLL PRINCESS

Tom Benn

Manchester, July 1996, the month after the IRA bomb. The *Evening News* reports two murders. On the front page is a photograph of an heiress to an oil fortune, her body discovered in the basement of a block of flats . . . Buried in the later pages there's a fifty-word piece on the murder of a young prostitute. For Bane, it's the latter that hits hardest. Determined to find out what happened to his childhood sweetheart, it soon becomes clear that the two stories belong on the same page, as Bane immerses himself in a world of drugs, gun arsenals, human trafficking and a Manchester in decay . . .